Dartmouth college. Class of

Decennial record of the class of 1877

Dartmouth college. Class of

Decennial record of the class of 1877

Reprint of the original, first published in 1877.

1st Edition 2024 | ISBN: 978-3-38612-136-1

Antigonos Verlag is an imprint of Outlook Verlagsgesellschaft mbH.

Verlag (Publisher): Outlook Verlag GmbH, Zeilweg 44, 60439 Frankfurt, Deutschland, info@outlook-verlag.de
Vertretungsberechtigt (Authorized to represent): E. Roepke, Zeilweg 44, 60439 Frankfurt, Deutschland
Druck (Print): Libri Plureos GmbH, Friedensallee 273, 22763 Hamburg, Deutschland

DECENNIAL RECORD

OF THE

CLASS OF 1877,

DARTMOUTH COLLEGE,

1877-1887.

HANOVER, N. H.
PRINTED AT THE DARTMOUTH PRESS,
1887.

Dear Classmates :—

After much delay, unavoidable so far as we are concerned, we present you this Decennial Record of the class. The plan upon which it is constructed has been already sufficiently outlined in our preliminary circular. In the case of the non-graduate members of the class, it covers more than ten years of time, as it seemed best to begin the record of these brethren with the date of their leaving the class.

In so far as the record herein given is imperfect, we submit that the blame, unless it be for lack of perseverance, should not fall upon us. The office of class secretary, never a sinecure, becomes more and more burdensome as the years go by. Not only does the amount of our own leisure time diminish, but the sad fact has become very apparent that the interest of our classmates in each other is growing less year by year, and it is yearly becoming more difficult to gather material for a report of this kind.

In the hope, however, that the following pages may serve to renew the pleasant memories of college days and to strengthen our regard for each other and to keep the memory green of those who have gone before, we have gladly contributed whatever labor was necessary in the preparation of this Record.

Cordially yours,

John M. Comstock,

August 15, 1887.   C. M. Goddard.

DECENNIAL RECORD

OF

DARTMOUTH '77.

CHARLES DARWIN ADAMS,
Springfield, Mo.

For the first two years after graduation he was principal of
the People's Academy and Morrisville Graded School, at Morrisville, Vt.   Entered Andover Theological Seminary in the fall
of 1879, and remained there two years, leaving at the close of
the middle year.   From 1881 to 1884 was instructor in Greek
and physics in Cushing Academy, Ashburnham, Mass., resigning his position there to accept an election to the chair of Greek
and Physics in Drury College, Springfield, Mo., his present location.   Was ordained an evangelist at Springfield, July 2, 1885,
and for some time supplied the pulpit of the Congregational
church at Riverdale, Mo.   Is now superintendent of the Congregational Sunday-School at Springfield.   Was married, Aug.
24, 1881, to Julia Amanda, daughter of David Stevens of Wilton,
N. H.   They have no children.

GEORGE ELWYN ATKINSON, son of Thomas and Emily
(Noyes) Atkinson, was born at Bolton, Mass., Sept. 8, 1852.
His father, a farmer, had died before our college days.   In 1867
his parents removed to Hudson, Mass., which was subsequently
his home.   His preparation for college was obtained at the Hudson High School, with one term at Wilbraham Wesleyan Academy.   He was thrown almost entirely on his own resources for
his education, and was diligently engaged in manual labor when
not with his class at Hanover.   His health, for some time not
strong, failed him during our senior year, and he was forced to
leave unfilled the position of Class Day poet, to which he had
been chosen by the class.   The summer following graduation

he spent in the woods of Maine, and returned in the fall with health apparently restored. It was a time of unusual sickness at Hudson, and for some weeks he devoted himself too closely to the care of the sick. In the winter he obtained a position on a Boston newspaper, but was soon obliged to give it up. Under medical advice, he spent several months on a farm at South Hampton, Nova Scotia, returning home in the following winter, somewhat benefited in health. From March to September, 1879, he was engaged in various out-door work for Daniel Whitcher, a lumber manufacturer of Landaff, N. H., and from Nov. 1879 till Jan. 1880 taught at Landaff. On finishing his school he began the study of law with Hon. A. P. Carpenter, at Bath, N. H., but a severe cold which he had contracted while teaching rapidly developed into consumption, and he was forced to give up study in March. On the 20th of April he was taken to Littleton, N. H., where his attending physician resided, and remained there until his death, May 10, 1880. Carpenter and Robinson were with him at the end, with his mother and sister, and they, together with Carrigan, Hammond, Saunderson, and Sewall, attended the funeral at Hudson. Diligent in labor, loyal and unselfish in friendship, of undoubted mental ability, no one of the class could have been more sincerely or deeply mourned than Atkinson.

GILBERT BROWNELL BALCH,

79 Milk St., Boston, Mass.

Studied law one year at the Boston University School of Law, and then, having made a change of plans, spent three years at Andover Theological Seminary, graduating there in 1881. Was ordained pastor of the Congregational church at Kingston, N. H., Aug. 4, 1881, and was dismissed by council from the pastorate, March 4, 1884, having been obliged to give up work by the breaking down of his health from nervous prostration. For three months was unable to do any work, and has since been engaged in the subscription book business. Canvassed for the first three months, traveled as field manager for six months, and then was in business for himself in partnership with his brother at Toronto, Ont., until last January. Since that date he has been a member of the firm of Martin Garrison & Co., subscription book publishers and dealers, doing business at the above address. Resides at 33 Wellington St. Was town superintendent of schools at Kingston in 1883. In politics calls himself an Independent, but not a Mugwump. Is a member of the Union Congregational church, Boston. Was married, July 14, 1881, at Georgetown, Mass., to Lizzie Sarah, daughter of the late R. Denis Perkins of Topsfield, Mass. They have no children.

GEORGE ADDISON BROWN,

Bellows Falls, Vt.

Immediately after graduation he entered the law office of J. D. Bridgman, at Bellows Falls, and in the fall of '77 entered Harvard Law School, where he remained one year. For three years from the fall of '78 he was principal of the Bellows Falls High School, meanwhile continuing his law studies, so that he was admitted to the Windham county bar in March 1881. In July 1881 he began practice at Bellows Falls, and has so remained. In the September election of 1880, he received the Republican nomination for representative to the state legislature, but was defeated at the polls after several ballotings. Was superintendent of schools for the town of Rockingham from 1883 to 1887, and is chairman of the board of school directors of the town for the present year, the town system of schools having been adopted at the last March election. Is now for the third year chairman of the board of village bailiffs. Was one of five delegates from Vermont at the Anti-saloon Republican Convention, held at Chicago in Sept. 1886, and was appointed to represent Vermont on the national committee of that organization, and is still acting in that capacity. Delivers frequent addresses on educational and temperance subjects, and has been a Memorial Day orator on two occasions. Is a member of the Sons of Temperance, has twice been Worthy Patriarch of the local division, and also Grand Worthy Patriarch for the state. Still a Republican in politics. Is an attendant at the Congregational church, and has twice been a member of the prudential committee of the society associated with it. Was married, July 18, 1877, to Flora E., daughter of Edson X. Pierce of Springfield, Vt. Their children are : Nelson Pierce (the class baby), born May 13, 1878; Ruth, born Dec. 1, 1882; James Barrett, born March 3, 1885.

ALFRED HILLS CAMPBELL,
Johnson, Vt.

For two years subsequent to graduation he was principal of Kingston Academy, Kingston, N. H., then for five years associate principal of Cushing Academy, Ashburnham, Mass., and since 1884 principal of the Vermont State Normal School, Johnson, Vt. Served on the examining committee at Dartmouth in 1885. Is one of the vice-presidents of the American Institute of Instruction for the present year. Is a Republican in politics and a member of the Congregational church at Johnson. Was married, Nov. 29, 1877, to Hattie E. Winchester of Westport, Mass. They have the following children: Arthur Winchester, born Sept. 12, 1878, died Dec. 29, 1878; Lillian Maud, born Oct. 9, 1880; Carroll Alfred, born June 5, 1882; Alice Cary, born March 27, 1887.

PHILIP CARPENTER,
38 Park Row, New York, N. Y.

Read law with his father, at Bath, N. H., from July 1877, and was admitted to the New Hampshire bar, at Concord, Sept. 2, 1880. From the tenth of that month till Sept. 1, 1881, he was in partnership with his father, at Bath. The latter then being appointed to the Bench, he practiced there alone till Jan. 15, 1882, when he became a member of the firm of Drew [D. C. 1870], Jordan & Carpenter, at Lancaster, N. H., to which place he removed April 15 following. In June 1885 he was admitted to the New York bar, and began practice there, removing there in September. Spent the summer of '86, from July to September, in a trip to Great Britain and the Continent. Was for some years a member of the Republican State Central Committee of New Hampshire, and in June 1885 was appointed by Gov. Currier Judge Advocate General on the governor's staff, with the rank of Brigadier General. Member of the Independent Order of Odd Fellows, and a Knight Templar in the North Star Commandery, F. and A. M., at Lancaster; also a member of the Association of the Bar of the City of New York, the Delta Kappa

Epsilon Club, and the Republican Club of the City of New York. He attends the Madison Square Presbyterian church ; his political proclivities are sufficiently indicated above. Was married, Sept. 3, 1880, at Winsted, Ct., to Fanny Hallock, daughter of Rev. Thomas H. Rouse of Makawao, Maui, Hawaiian Islands. No children.

EDWARD CHARLES CARRIGAN,

6 Ashburton Place, Boston, Mass.

Traveled through Vermont and New Hampshire as a reporter for the *Boston Globe* from graduation to March 1878, and from that time till October 1879 was manager of the Passumpsic and Connecticut Valley News Department on the *Boston Journal.* Since that time he has done a large amount of journalistic work in connection with several of the Boston dailies. For a time he maintained a nominal connection with the law office of Farr & Stevens, Littleton, N. H., and since October 1879 has been enrolled as a law student in Gen. B. F. Butler's office. Was principal of the Blossom Street Evening School, in Boston, from the fall of 1879 till January 1882, and of the Evening High School from the last date till September 1886. Was nominated by Gov. Butler and confirmed by the Council, May 31, 1883, as a member of the State Board of Education, the term of office being eight years. Represented the state of Massachusetts on appointment of the Governor as delegate to the Interstate Educational Convention held at Louisville, Ky., in September 1883. Was largely instrumental in procuring the passage, by the Massachusetts Legislature of 1886, of a bill obliging cities of 50,000 inhabitants or over to maintain evening high schools, and another bill to strengthen the tenure of office of teachers, which allows the cities and towns of the state to dispense, at their option, with the annual election of teachers. Was presented by the Boston Schoolmasters, Nov. 2, 1886, with a gold watch, chain, and Phi Beta Kappa key, as a token of their appreciation of his services in the tenure of office matter. Was in Europe several weeks in the summer and fall of 1886 for business and travel. Has been during the past year connected with the Boston University School of Law, and graduated there in June last. Expects to be admitted to the bar in a few months. Is chairman of a committee of the American Institute of Instruction (appointed in 1886) relative to securing federal aid to common schools. Member of the Boston Press Club, The Clefs, Massachusetts Schoolmasters' Club, and a life member of the Boston Schoolmasters' Association. Is secretary of the Boston Association of Dartmouth Alumni. In politics, classes himself as a Butler Independent. Unmarried.

FRANKLIN MUNROE CHAPIN,

Tientsin, China.

Spent the first three years after graduation as a student at Hartford Theological Seminary, graduating there in 1880. Was accepted for missionary service by the American Board, and assigned to the North China mission. Was ordained May 20, 1880, in the Second Congregational church at Keene, N. H., and sailed from San Francisco Sept. 1. Was stationed for some years at Kalgan, but is now at Pang Chuang. The post-office address of the mission, however, is as given above. His occasional letters printed in the *Missionary Herald* give a graphic account of his work. Has in preparation, to be issued from the press soon in the Chinese language, an article on Confucianism and Christianity, which he kindly offers to send your secretary for reviewing. Was married, June 30, 1880, to Flora M., daughter of William A. Barrett of Keene, N. H. William Sanders Chapin was born at Peking, May 12, 1881, and another son, whose name is unreported, at Kalgan in November 1883.

IRA ARTHUR CHASE,

Bristol, N. H.

In the fall and winter of 1877–8 he was principal of the Graded School at Bristol, N. H., and during the following spring and summer read law with Lewis W. Fling of Bristol. In the fall of 1878 he was principal of the Orleans Liberal Institute, at Glover, Vt., and in February and March 1879 temporary assistant in the New Hampton (N. H.) Literary Institution. During the school year 1879–80 he was again in charge of the Bristol Graded School. Meanwhile he continued the study of law, and was admitted to the New Hampshire bar on examination, at Con.

'cord, March 17, 1881. Has since practiced at Bristol. Was assistant clerk of the New Hampshire Senate in 1883 and 1885, and clerk in 1887. Has been a member of the local board of health and school board, and town treasurer, and is a member of the corporation of the Bristol Savings Bank. Is a Mason, and has been master of the local lodge and member of the chapter and council. Member of the New Hampshire Antiquarian Society. In politics a Republican. Member of the Bristol Congregational church, and clerk of the society connected with it. Was married, July 6, 1881, to Abby Maria, daughter of Cyrus Taylor of Bristol. They have no children.

WILLIAM FOLSOM CHASE,[1]
Laconia, N. H.

Entered the employ of S. E. Young & Co., jewelers, at Laconia, N. H., in October 1877, and servedt here an apprenticeship of three years, after the expiration of which he remained with the firm till May 1883. From the next fall till March 1, 1887, he was at the head of the crockery and upholstery department in the mercantile establishment of O'Shea Brothers, at Laconia. Since the last date he has been in business for himself, as a dealer in books, stationery, and fancy goods. A Republican in politics. Was married in Manchester, N. H., May 21, 1881, to Eva R., daughter of Benjamin C. Badger of Laconia. They have one daughter, Margery, born Sept. 26, 1885.

GEORGE HENRY CHILD,
Harper's Ferry, W. Va.

In the fall of 1878 he entered the employ of the wholesale dry goods house of Morgan, Root & Co., Cleveland, O., and remained there till 1885, the firm having become Root & McBride Bros. in 1884, and with Taylor, Kilpatrick & Co., in the same business, to January 1886. From January to March of that year he was with E. C. Shaw & Co., Toledo, O., at which latter date he was called to his old home, at Harper's Ferry, W. Va., by his father's illness, and has since remained there as manager of a a general store. A Republican in politics, and without religious preference. Unmarried.

John Moore Comstock,
Chelsea, Vt.

Was a resident graduate at Hanover for the first year after graduation, and was considerably engaged in private tutoring. Taught at Chelsea, Vt., in the fall of 1878, and then from December 1878 to April 1879 was editorial assistant on the *Republican Observer*, at White River Junction, Vt. His home was then at Chelsea from May 1879, and he was engaged in teaching there with some intermission from September 1879 till November 1882. Was principal of the High School at Springfield, Vt., from March 1883 to June 1884, and instructor in languages in the Vermont Episcopal Institute, at Burlington, Vt., from December 1884 till June 1885. The death of his father, in July 1885, caused him to remain in Chelsea, and he has been principal of Chelsea Academy since April 1886. Was town superintendent of schools from April 1881 to March 1883, and is county treasurer for the two years beginning Dec. 1, 1886. Has been statistical secretary of the Alumni Association of Dartmouth College since 1881 ; is a member of the Vermont Historical Society. Has edited the following published pamphlets : Eight Annual Reports of the Class of 1877, besides this Decennial Record ; eleven annual issues of the *Obituary Record of the Graduates of Dartmouth College*, pp. 209 in all ; *General Catalogue of Dartmouth College*, 1880, pp. 208 ; *Supplement to the General Catalogue of Dartmouth College*, 1885, pp. 56 ; *Address List of the Alumni of Dartmouth College*, 1882, pp. 55 ; *Catalogue of the New Hampshire Alpha of the Phi Beta Kappa*, 1884, pp. 74 ; another edition of the same, 1887, pp. 76 ; also the greater part of a *Manual of the Congregational Church in Chelsea, Vermont*, 1882, pp. 63. In politics is a Republican, but a rather unreliable one. Is a member of the Congregational church of Chelsea, member of its standing committee, superintendent of its Sunday-School, and clerk of the ecclesiastical society connected therewith. Was married, Aug. 24, 1881, to Persis Sylvia, daughter of Dea. Franklin Dearborn of Chelsea. Their children are as follows: Harold Dearborn, born June 13, 1882 ; Catherine, born Aug. 18, 1884, died Aug. 26, 1884 ; Donald Laird, born Oct. 17, 1885 ; Margaret, born Jan. 24, 1887.

CHARLES HERMANCE COOPER,
Northfield, Minn.

In September 1877 he took charge of the Abbott Grammar School, in Washington, D. C., but resigned in the ensuing winter and returned to New England, taking charge of the High School at East Longmeadow, Mass., during the spring of '78. During the summer he attended the Sauveur School of Languages at Amherst. For the year following he served as assistant in the Hitchcock Free High School, Brimfield, Mass., and then, being promoted to the principalship, remained in that capacity three years. The year 1882–3 he spent as tutor at Dartmouth, having charge of the freshman Greek and the history of freshman and sophomore years. In the spring of 1883 he was elected to the chair of History and Political Science in Carleton College, Northfield, Minn., where he began work in the ensuing fall, and where he still remains. He is connected with the First Congregational church of Northfield, being a member of its prudential committee and assistant superintendent of its Sunday-School; politically, he wishes to be classed as a Mugwump. He was married at North Woburn, Mass., Jan. 10, 1883, to Caroline Antoinette, daughter of the late Rev. Melancthon G. Wheeler of Woburn. They have one daughter, Helen, born July 24, 1884.

ALBERT GLENMORE COX,
Essex, Vt.

Was principal of the Vermont Liberal Institute, Plymouth Uuion, Vt., in the fall of '77, of the Cavendish (Vt.) Graded School in the ensuing winter, and again at Plymouth Union in the spring of '78. From the fall of '78 to the spring of '80 traveled most of the time as insurance agent, also farming a little. Was again principal of the Vermont Liberal Institute from the spring of 1880 till the close of the spring term of 1881. From 1881 to 1886 was principal of the New Hampton Institution, Fairfax, Vt., and since the fall of 1886 of the Essex Classical Institute, Essex, Vt. Has meanwhile been enrolled as a law student with T. O. Seaver of Woodstock, Vt., and is nearly ready to apply for admission to the bar. Was town superintendent of schools at Fairfax from April 1883 to April 1886. Is president of the Essex Village Improvement Society. A Republican in politics. A member of the Baptist church at Essex, and superintendent of its Sunday-School. Was married, Dec. 5, 1881, to Viola S., daughter of Rowland Maxham of Bridgewater, Vt. They have no children.

REUBEN MELVILLE CRAMER,

111 West 34th St., New York, N. Y.

Was a city reporter on the *New York Times* in the summer of 1877, and for a year from the ensuing fall was principal of the Hearne (Texas) Academy, doing some work also on the *Hearne Courier.* He then studied medicine at the University of Pennsylvania, and at the College of Physicians and Surgeons of New York, graduating at the latter in the spring of 1881. From the spring of 1880 till the following October he was house physician and surgeon at the Hudson County Hospital, Jersey City, N. J., and for some time thereafter house surgeon at the Sailors' Retreat Hospital, Staten Island. From the spring of 1881 till December 1882 he held a similar position at Mt. Sinai Hospital, New York, and has since been in private practice in that city. In 1883 he reported himself as instructor in surgery in the New York Polyclinic Medical School, and as connected with the Manhattan Eye and Ear Hospital. Supposed to be still a Democrat and unmarried.

WILLIAM GAGE DAVIS,

Mills Building, 15 Broad St., New York, N. Y.

Took the two years' course in Columbia Law School, from which he graduated in May 1879. Has since been in practice in New York city, having been for some time with Dos Passos Brothers, at the above address. Is a Republican and a member of the Pilgrim Congregational church, New York. Was married in New York city, Sept. 14, 1886, to E. F., daughter of the late John D. Farrington.

CHARLES LOMBARD DAY, son of the Rev. Dr. Pliny Butts and Mary B. (Chapin) Day, was born at Hollis, N. H., April 28,

1854. His father, a graduate of Amherst in 1834, was a Congregational pastor in Derry, N. H., and finally at Hollis, where he died in 1869. He was also a trustee of Dartmouth from 1863 to his death. After Dr. Day's death, the family returned to Derry, where our classmate was partially fitted for college at Pinkerton Academy. In 1871 they removed to Grinnell, Iowa, which was Day's home for the remainder of his life. He was there connected with Iowa College, in the Preparatory Department and for one year in the college proper, joining our class at the beginning of our sophomore year. In the fall after graduation he was instructor in the English Language and Literature in the Michigan Military Academy, at Orchard Lake, Mich., and in the ensuing winter began the study of law at Grinnell, in the office of Haines & Lyman. He spent the year 1878-9 in the Law Department of the State University of Iowa, at Iowa City, graduating there in June 1879, and being admitted to the bar at the same time. He was intending to return to Iowa City for further study, but was taken with typho-malarial fever, which resulted in his death, at his home in Grinnell, Sept. 20, 1879, after an illness of about two weeks. For a long time he had been hampered in his work by a weakness of the heart, and it was the failure of this organ that finally caused his death. Naturally reserved, and a close student, we did not know him so well in college as many of the class were known, but he was highly respected by us all, and his early death caused sincere grief.

CLIFTON SLATE DEANE,

Prattville, Ala.

Was teacher of mathematics and sciences in Lawrence Academy, Groton, Mass., for the first year after graduation. In the summer of '78 studied chemistry at the Summer School of Science at Cambridge, Mass. In the fall ensuing he had charge of a High School at Sheffield, Mass., and was then at home (Bernardston, Mass.) till August 1879. At that date he went to Grundy Center, Iowa, where he taught in the fall, and for the next six years had charge of various public schools in Grundy and Marshall counties, in that state, with now and then an "excursion" into the book business, and some other lines. Was principal of the Fayette County Male and Female Institute, at Fayette C. H., Ala., for the school year 1885–6, and has been since the fall of 1886 principal of the Prattville (Ala.) Male and Female Academy, and superintendent of the public schools of Prattville. Has acted of late with the Democratic party. Is a member of a Congregational church. Unmarried.

CHARLES ROLLIN DUSTIN,

74 Sagamore St., Manchester, N. H.

Taught at New Boston, N. H., in the fall of 1877, at Wellfleet, Mass., in the ensuing winter, and in the spring of 1878 a Grammar School in Manchester, N. H. From the fall of 1878 he read law for about two years and a half in the office of John H. Andrews, in Manchester, and has since been clerk for the John Hoyt Co., paper manufacturers, the firm being now known as the Amoskeag Paper Co. Was married, June 13, 1885, to Hattie May, daughter of William C. Knowlton of Manchester. A son was born March 6, 1886, but lived but a short time.

CHARLES WINTHROP EAGER,

776 Elm St., Manchester, N. H.

Has been book-keeper for Eager & Rand, grocers, in Manchester, for most of the time since graduation. Read law for a time with Hon. H. E. Burnham [D. C. 1865]. Was a member of the city Common Council in 1878, 1879, and 1880, and an Alderman in 1887. Was a member of the New Hampshire House of Representatives in 1881, serving on the Committee on Elections. A member of the Derryfield Club; Republican in politics. Was married, Dec. 16, 1886, to Jennie S. Williams of Manchester.

EUGENE LESLIE EMERY,

Grand Forks, Dak.

Entered the law office of Copeland & Edgerly, Great Falls, N. H., Aug. 13, 1877. Was principal of a Grammar School at Hampton, N. H., in the winter of 1877–8, and taught at Newington, N. H., in the winter of 1878–9. Left Great Falls late in

1879, and was a student in the office of Brooks, Camirand & Hurd, at Sherbrooke, Que., from Dec. 22, 1879, till Aug. 28, 1880. Was then for one year principal of the Frelighsburg (Que.) Academy, and for the fall and winter of 1881–2 of the Barton (Vt.) Academy and Graded School. Was admitted to the bar of Orleans county, at Irasburg, Vt., Feb. 12, 1882, and opened an office at Grand Forks, Dak., March 28. He gradually worked into the loan business, the first year acting as agent for the Red River Loan and Trust Co. of Fargo, and later on his own account. In 1885 he visited New Hampshire and organized the New England Investment Co., which was incorporated Aug. 12, 1885. Of this company he is secretary and general manager, having entire charge of the business. Sumner Wallace is a director of the company, and has been largely interested in its operations. Emery has been since its organization (March 1885) a director of the Grand Forks National Bank. Is a Democrat in politics, and was secretary of the Democratic city committee during the year 1886. Attends the Presbyterian church. Was married, Oct. 30, 1883, to Isabel M., daughter of Rufus I. Stevens of Great Falls, N. H. They have no children.

FRED WINSLOW FARNSWORTH,
Red Wing, Minn.

Has been since graduation principal of the High School at Red Wing. Is a Republican in politics, and one of Service's parishioners in the First Presbyterian church of Red Wing. Was married in the spring of 1885, and has two children—both girls —one born May 5, 1886, and the other May 24, 1887. He has not reported the names of wife or children.

CHARLES BARTLETT HAMMOND,
Nashua, N. H.

Spent the first three years after graduation in Harvard Medical School, graduating in June 1880, and has been in practice in Nashua since Oct. 1, 1880. Was married, Oct. 16, 1883, to Mary Louisa, daughter of Dr. William A. Tracy of Nashua. A son died in the spring of 1885, at the age of eleven months.

John DeForest Haskell,
Stromsburg, Neb.

In the fall of 1877 began the study of law with Hatch & Parkinson [D. C. 1870], in Cincinnati, O., but an attack of typhoid fever soon compelled him to come home to recruit, and he remained there the rest of the year. Studied at Harvard Law School in 1878-9, and at Boston University in 1879-80, graduating at the latter in 1880. Practiced at Norfolk, Neb., in the firm of Haskell & Sattler, from 1880 to 1884, being county attorney some time from the spring of 1882. Has since been at Stromsburg, Neb., as president of the Park Bank, established Sept. 9, 1884. Is vicepresident of the Stromsburg Board of Trade, a Mason, a Republican, and in religious preference a Congregationalist, though a trustee of a Presbyterian church. Was married, May 20, 1885, to Nellie Trumbull, daughter of William Mathewson of South Woodstock, Ct. They have a son, Cornelius DeForest, the date of whose birth has not been reported.

John Edward Ingham,
327 Jackson St., St. Paul, Minn.

Was appointed receiver to wind up the affairs of the Park Place Hotel, in St. Paul, July 27, 1877, and managed the hotel until Nov. 9. Two days after, he entered the employ of Ingham & Corlies, manufacturers of doors, sash and blinds. With the intention of learning the business, he began near the bottom of the ladder, as teamster. In about a year he became salesman, and in February 1879 the business was left in his hands for about two months, and after that he was head salesman, and business manager in the absence of Mr. Corlies, the office partner. In January 1881 the firm became Corlies, Chapman & Drake, and he remained with them till 1884, being most of the time in charge of their manufacturing department. From March 20, 1884, till March 1886, he was in the same line of business for himself, being vice-president of the Taylor & Craig Company, in which firm he had one-third interest. In June 1886 he bought out the stock of E. Lytle, dealer in watches, diamonds, and jewelry, and has since followed this business successfully. Is a Mason, a Republican, and an attendant at Christ church (Episcopal). Was married, July 3, 1883, to Anna B., daughter of Isaac Banker of St. Paul. Their children are Helen Marion, born April 30, 1884, and Edith Belle, born Oct. 31, 1885.

JOHN SAVILLIAN LADD,

Sistof, Bulgaria.

Studied for three years in Union Theological Seminary, graduating May 10, 1880. Was ordained deacon and elder of the Methodist Episcopal church by Bishop Willey, in New York, April 4, 1880, and joined the New York Conference. Was appointed missionary to Bulgaria, and sailed from New York June 12. Was stationed at Sistof till April 1883, and was then for a year at Rustchuck, in charge of the book business of the mission. Has since been at Sistof, in charge of a theological school. Was married at Philippopolis, May 24, 1881, to Rosa Doolittle, a graduate of Oberlin in '75, and a missionary teacher. They are said to have had one child, not now living. Ladd has not reported of late.

CHARLES EDWARD LESLIE,

Waseca, Minn.

Read law with his father, C. B. Leslie, at Wells River, Vt., from Sept. 1, 1877, and was admitted to the Orange county bar, at Chelsea, June 7, 1879. Went to Minnesota in the latter part of July, and soon located in practice at Waterville, removing to Waseca, Jan. 1, 1880, where he has since practiced. Was city attorney from May 1881 to May 1882, and again since May 1887. Was judge of the municipal court by appointment of the governor, from August 1885 to May 1886. Unsuccessful candidate for county attorney on the Prohibition ticket in 1886. Hardly knows whether to call himself a Democrat or a Prohibitionist. A member of the Congregational church at Waseca. Was married, May 1, 1882, to Martha Josephine, daughter of Samuel S. Comee of Waseca. Their children are: Charles Comee, born Aug. 28, 1883 ; Myron Frederick, born Sept. 5, 1885 ; Ruth Elizabeth, born July 15, 1887.

John Crego Lester,
406 Clinton St., Brooklyn, N. Y.

Taught at Goshen, Ct., in the fall and winter of 1877–8. Studied medicine at the Long Island College Hospital, Brooklyn, from the spring of 1878, graduating there June 27, 1879. In the following month he was appointed assistant physician at the Kings County Lunatic Asylum, in Brooklyn. Resigned in a few months to accept an appointment as medical superintendent of the Inebriates' Home, at Fort Hamilton, N. Y. Left there early in 1881, and has since been engaged in general practice in Brooklyn. Since 1882 he has been editor of the *American Medical Digest*, monthly. Is a Mason, a member of the American Legion of Honor, the Royal Arcanum, and the Knights of Honor, and surgeon general of the National Provident Union. Member of the Medical Society of the County of Kings. Head physician to the Southern Dispensary and Hospital in Brooklyn. In politics a "*quasi* Democrat," and was president of the South Brooklyn Independent Club in the campaign of 1884. A Congregationalist in religious preference. Was married, June 24, 1880, to Octavia, daughter of Noah S. Wadhams of Goshen, Ct. They have no children.

Charles Edwin Lord,
Franklin, Pa.

In the fall and winter of 1877–8 he was principal of the Charlestown, N. H., High School, and in the succeeding spring, summer, and fall traveled as canvasser through Southern New Hampshire and Vermont. In the winter of '78–9 he taught at East Lebanon, N. H., and then from the last of February to the last of April was in collection business in Boston. Served as principal of the High School at Saugus, Mass., in the spring of '79, and was then till Sept. 1, 1880, traveling agent for Sheldon & Co.'s school publications. Was in charge of a Grammar School at Vineyard Haven, Mass., in the fall of 1880, and at South Chatham, Mass., in the following winter. From March 1 to July 1, 1881, he was classical teacher in Temple Grove Ladies' Seminary, Saratoga Springs, N. Y.; from Aug. 1, 1881, to March 1, 1883, head master of the Weston Military Institute,

Weston, Ct., and then till Sept. 1 principal of the last-named school. Was then classical master in the Yeates Institute, Lancaster, Pa., for one year, and for two years engaged in private tutoring in Newport, R. I. His present position in charge of the High School at Franklin, Pa., he assumed in the fall of 1886. Politically, he is a Mugwump; to the question regarding religious preference he declares himself to be "a member of the Protestant Episcopal church, and a firm believer in the doctrine of evolution as held by John Fiske." He was married at Vineyard Haven, Mass., May 21, 1885, to Annie Franklin, daughter of Capt. Grafton L. Daggett of Vineyard Haven. A daughter, Constance, was born Oct. 20, 1886.

JOHN MERRIAM,
New Milford, Susquehanna Co., Pa.

Spent the first three years after graduation in Andover Theological Seminary, graduating there in 1880. For a time during his senior year there he supplied the pulpit of the Congregational church at Dracut, Mass. For three months from Sept. 1880 he was acting pastor of the Presbyterian church at North Platte, Neb. Went from there to New Hampton, Ia., and began work there with the Congregational church, being ordained May 19, 1881. Left there in the latter part of January, 1882, and went to New York, giving his time to post-graduate study in Union Theological Seminary till the term closed, in May. Went directly to Harford, Pa., where he remained with the Congregational church till Nov. 1884. From Nov. 9, 1884, to May 1887, was pastor of the Bennet Presbyterian church, at Luzerne, Pa., and since the last date of a church of the same denomination at New Milford, Pa. A Republican in politics. Unmarried.

HENRY LYNN MOORE,
245 Hennepin Ave., Minneapolis, Minn.

Went to Lake City, Minn., August 1877, as principal of the High School; at the end of the first year was elected superintendent of schools, and continued in that position till Feb. 1882. From that date till the following June he was principal of the Washington School in Minneapolis, at the last date being chosen assistant superintendent of schools.   Held this position till June 1886, being acting superintendent most of the time till Jan. 1884, in the absence of the superintendent as U. S. Consul at Trieste and afterwards at Leipsic.   In June 1886 the office of assistant was merged in the superintendency, and he permanently left the profession of teaching.   Is now in the real estate and loan business, in the firm of Spear & Moore.   Is a member of the Ancient Order of United Workmen, and a Master Workman in the same; Secretary of the Dartmouth Association of the Northwest.   Republican in politics; a member of the Plymouth Congregational church, Minneapolis.   Was married, Dec. 25, 1879, to Nettie, daughter of Hiram Center of Lake City.   They have two children,—Guernsey Center, born Jan. 7, 1881, and Edith, born Nov. 8, 1883.

WILLIS EMERSON NOXON,
27 Washington Ave. South, Minneapolis, Minn.

He was principal of the Graded School at Housatonic, Mass., through the fall and winter of 1877–8.   In the spring of '78 he began the study of law with H. C. Joynes, at Great Barrington, Mass., but his eyes failed, and he resumed teaching in the fall, as superintendent of schools at Port Jefferson, N. Y., where he remained two years.   He held a similar position at Plainview, Minn., from 1880 to 1882, and then, having continued his law studies while teaching, took a year in the Law School of the University of Michigan, and after graduating there in April 1883, opened an office in Minneapolis, in the firm of Noxon & Benton, where he still remains.   Unmarried.   "In politics a Mugwump; my religion embraces the whole human race and the planetary system."

FREDERICK LANGDON OWEN, JR.,
Canton, Mass.

Read law with C. A. Dole, Lebanon, N. H., from July to November, 1877, long enough to satisfy him that the profession was not to his taste.   Was then principal of the Grammar School at Dennis Port, Mass., from Dec. 2, 1877, to Sept. 20, 1878, and then in a school of the same grade at Harwich, Mass., from Dec. 2 to Dec. 27, 1878. Then was at Canton, Mass., at the head of a Graded School, from Dec. 30, 1878, to April 1881. Then went to Franklin Falls, N. H., as principal of a High School, but was recalled to Canton the same week to take the principalship of the High School there. In this position he remains. A member of the High School Masters' Club, meeting monthly in Boston. A Republican, and an attendant at a Congregational church. Was married, Dec. 28, 1881, to Emma Poelien, daughter of William Bense of Canton. No children.

OSCAR JOSEPH PFEIFFER,
Denver, Colo.

For the three years immediately following our graduation he had charge of the Graded School at Lancaster, N. H., and for the next three was a member of Harvard Medical School. Rowed on the Harvard University crew of 1881. On going to Boston, became assistant to Carrigan in the Blossom St. Evening School, and on the latter's promotion became principal of the same, Jan. 24, 1882. In October 1882 he began a connection with the Massachusetts General Hospital, which continued until August 1, 1884, he finishing his service as senior house surgeon. In June 1884 he received his medical degree. From August to November he kept an office in Boston, and at the latter date received the appointment which he still holds as Medical Director of the Union Pacific Railway Co., with headquarters at Denver. A member of the Massachusetts Medical Society. In politics usually acts with the Republican party; as to religious preference has nothing to answer. Was married in New York city, Nov. 8, 1884, to Annie Hale, daughter of Samuel G. Folsom of Portsmouth, N. H. No children.

WILLIAM WARREN PRESCOTT,
Battle Creek, Mich.

He was principal of the Graded School at Northfield, Vt., for two years, and then for one year principal of the Montpelier (Vt.) Union School. From June 1880 till April 1, 1882, he was editor and part owner of the Biddeford, Me., *Union and Journal,* and from the last date till July 24, 1885, editor and proprietor of the *Vermont Watchman*, Montpelier, Vt.   Upon leaving Montpelier he became president of Battle Creek College, at Battle Creek, Mich., his present position.   Only offices reported are, member of the school board at Montpelier, and trustee of the Seventh Day Adventist Educational Society at Battle Creek. Acts with the Republican party, when with any ; member of the Seventh Day Adventist church of Battle Creek.   Was married at Penacook, N. H., July 8, 1880, to Sarah Frances, daughter of J. P. Sanders.   No children.

ANGUS ARCHIBALD ROBERTSON,
199 Willoughby Ave., Brooklyn, N. Y.

Spent the first year after graduation in Yale Theological Seminary, then transferring his relations to Oberlin Seminary, where he graduated in June 1880.   Soon after he began work with the Congregational church at South Haven, Mich., and was ordained to the ministry there Nov. 4, 1880.   Left there in the fall of 1881 on account of malaria.   After remaining for some time in and about Chicago, under medical treatment, he became pastor at Buda, Ill., the first of October, 1881, and remained there till the first of November, 1882.   The ensuing winter he spent in Portland, Me., and was then pastor of the Second Congregational church at Massena, N. Y., from May 1883 to June 1884.   In July following he began work at Vergennes, Vt., and was installed pastor Aug. 26.   Was dismissed by council, after a very successful pastorate, April 26, 1887, and left there May 3.   Spent the summer with a brother at Medford, Mass., and meanwhile accepted a call to the Willoughby Avenue Congregational church of Brooklyn, where at the date of his last letter he was expecting to begin work the middle of August. Was town superintendent of schools at Vergennes from April 1886 to April 1887.   A Republican in politics.   He was married, Sept. 16, 1880, to Mary Barrows, daughter of William C. How of Portland, Me.   As this Record goes to press, comes the sad news of Mrs. Robertson's death, at Medford, on the first of August.   She leaves one son, William Lord How, born April 2, 1883.

Benjamin Franklin Robinson,
Littleton, N. H.

Was the first two years after graduation principal of the High School at Littleton, and then entered upon the drug business there in the firm of Robinson Brothers. From Jan. 1, 1881, to May 1, 1887, was of the firm of Robinson & Goold, editors and proprietors of *The Littleton Journal,* a weekly newspaper. At the last date the paper changed hands, and Robinson has not reported his present business or prospects. Was elected a member of the Littleton Board of Education in the winter of 1880 for a term of three years, and was re-elected in 1883 and 1886. Was also superintendent of schools for the year 1885, and was appointed last spring collector of taxes for the town. Is a Mason, having taken the degrees to and including Knight Templar; has been Prelate of St. Gerard Commandery of Littleton. Republican in politics. He was married, Dec. 24, 1879, to E. Addie, daughter of the late Edward Kilburn of Littleton. Their children are : Fred Kilburn, born July 23, 1881, died April 27, 1882 ; Edward Kilburn, born April 16, 1883 ; Frank Owen, born Dec. 6, 1886.

Lewis Rosenthal,
20 Irving Place, New York, N. Y.

Went abroad in the summer of 1877, and was located in Paris till December 1881, when he returned to New York. While there was a student of philology and literature at the Sorbonne and the Collège de France, a student of law with Hon. E. F. Noyes [D. C. 1857], United States Minister to France, a private tutor, a contributor to various newspapers, and assistant secretary of the Franco-Texan Land Company. Since returning to New York he has been engaged in various literary and journalistic work, the latter chiefly in connection with the *Times* and *World.* Is the author of the following book, published in May 1882 by Henry Holt & Co. : *America and France ; the Influence of the United States on France in the Eighteenth Century,*—also of *Rousseau in Philadelphia* (pp. 10), in the *Magazine of American History* for July 1884. Has not reported in person for a long time, but is supposed to be still a Democrat and unmarried.

John Andrew Rowell,
Brainerd, Minn.

Left the class at the end of junior year, and spent the next two years on a farm at Chichester, N. H., teaching also for a part of the time. In September 1878 he entered Bangor Theological Seminary in the middle class, graduating there June 2, 1880. In that month began work at Weare, N. H., under appointment from the New Hampshire Home Missionary Society, and was ordained pastor of the Congregational church at South Weare, Oct. 14, 1880. Was dismissed from the pastorate by council, Dec. 7, 1882, having accepted a call to Francestown, N. H., and remained at Francestown till Nov. 1, 1886. He then went to Minnesota on invitation of the Superintendent of the Minneapolis Home Missionary Society, with the intention of doing home missionary work, but soon accepted a call to the First Congregational church of Brainerd, beginning work there Dec. 5, 1886. Edited a *Report of the Dedicatory Exercises of the Congregational Church Edifice, Francestown, N. H., July 1st*, 1884, pp. 23. At the last college commencement, he was given the degree of Bachelor of Arts by vote of the trustees and restored to his class, and in consequence will hereafter be regarded as a graduate member of the class. In politics is a Prohibitionist. Was married, July 5, 1875, to Alma Narcissa, daughter of Albert Holmes of Hopkinton, N. H. Their children are: Wilfrid Asa, born March 5, 1877; Marion Eliza, born April 18, 1879; Florence May, born July 31, 1881: Paul Albert, born July 24, 1882, died Sept. 15, 1883; Maurice Holmes, born Aug. 13, 1884.

George William Saunderson,
218 Columbus Ave., Boston, Mass.

Read law one year from September 1887 with George B. French [D. C. 1872], at Nashua, N. H. During the next two years he was a member of the Law School of Boston University, where he graduated in June 1880, also being in the offices of N. W. Ladd [D. C. 1873] and J. H. Hardy [D. C. 1870], in Boston. Was admitted to the Massachusetts bar in May 1880, and practiced in Boston from January 1881 to September 1883. His health having failed, he then gave up practice and went to California.   After traveling through the state for some time, in January 1884 he bought a small fruit ranch near Santa Barbara, and remained there till the summer of 1886.   Since the fall of 1886 he has been studying in the Monroe College of Oratory, in Boston.   Expects to remain there for another year, and then to make the teaching of the Monroe system his profession.   Is a member of the A. O. U. W. ; in politics a Republican, with Mugwump tendencies; a member of a Congregational church.   Unmarried.

ROBERT JOHN SERVICE,

Red Wing, Minn.

Became principal of the High School at Ottumwa, Iowa, in the fall of 1877, resigning in November 1878 to become private secretary to the assistant superintendent of the Chicago, Burlington & Quincy R. R., at Burlington, Iowa.   Left this position Aug. 20, 1879, and entered Union Theological Seminary, where he graduated in May 1882.   Spent several months in European travel in the summers of 1881 and '82.   Remained at the seminary for a year of post-graduate study, and in August 1883 located at Red Wing with the First Presbyterian church, over which he was ordained pastor by presbytery, Oct. 25, 1883.   Was married, Sept. 2, 1884, to Mary Duncan, daughter of Thomas McIlwraith of Hamilton, Ont.

JOHN LADD SEWALL,

Milton, Vt.

He was for two years principal of the Preparatory Department of Olivet College, Olivet, Mich., and then spent three years in Andover Theological Seminary, where he graduated in June 1882.   He began preaching at once at Westminster, Vt., and was ordained pastor of the Congregational church there July 19. He resigned in the spring of 1885, and was formally dismissed by council, April 21.   Began work with the church at Milton, Vt., the first of June following, and was installed pastor March 10, 1886.   Has done considerable reporting for the *Boston Journal* and *Globe*, and editorial work on the *Vermont Chronicle* and Chicago *Advance.*   An open letter of his to the Brattleboro Independents, printed in the Brattleboro *Phœnix* of Aug. 12, 1884, *almost* persuaded your secretary to vote for Blaine! Was scribe of the Convention of Congregational Ministers and Churches of Vermont, held at St. Albans in June 1884, and is now first Vice-President of the state organization of the Young People's Society of Christian Endeavor. In politics, there is no question as to his Republicanism. Was married at Littleton, Mass., Oct. 31, 1883, to Katharine Mussey, daughter of Shattuck Hartwell of Littleton, and reports as children, Mary Burnham, born Sept. 2, 1885, and Katharine Mussey, born Sept. 29, 1886.

ALBERT KIMBALL SMITH,
154 Public Square, Cleveland, O.

Read law from the summer of 1877 to the spring of 1879 with Austin DeWolf of Greenfield, Mass., teaching in the spring of 1878 at Hinsdale, N. H. He then decided to give up the law, and studied medicine from September 1879 with Dr. H. F. Biggar of Cleveland, O., and at Cleveland Homeopathic Medical College, where he graduated in March 1881. Was then in practice with Dr. Biggar till April 1882, and removed to Bellaire, Ohio, in May 1882. In the spring of 1885 he returned to Cleveland, and has since remained there. Is surgeon to the Cleveland Workhouse and the House of Refuge and Correction. A Republican in politics. Was married, June 28, 1883, to Ella Over of Bellaire.

JUSTIN HARVEY SMITH,
7, 9, and 13 Tremont Place, Boston, Mass.

From July 1877 to Jan. 1878 he was private secretary to John D. Philbrick, LL.D., [D. C. 1842], Superintendent of Schools of Boston. From February to July, 1878, he served as secretary of the United States Educational Exhibit at the Paris Exposition, of which Mr. Philbrick had been appointed superintendent, and in that capacity sailed from New York in March. After the expiration of this engagement he spent several months in European travel, returning to America in October. From Oct. 1877 to Feb. 1879 he was also principal of the Neponset Evening School. From Oct. 1878 to Feb. 1879 he was secretary of the Boston University School of Oratory, also a student there, and somewhat engaged in private tutoring, and then from February to July superintendent of schools at Malden, Mass. From Sept. 1879 to May 1881 he studied at Union Theological Seminary, New York, doing at the same time considerable private tutoring, and assisting Mrs. Martha J. Lamb in the preparation of her history of New York city. Being compelled by a throat trouble to relinquish or at least postpone his plans for a professional career, he served from May 1881 to Feb. 1883 as New· York agent for the educational publications of Charles Scribner's Sons, and from February to June as Chicago agent for the same firm. The firm then closed up their school-book department, and he at once took charge of the New York agency of Ginn, Heath & Co., remaining there till July 1884, when he was promoted to be manager of the home (Boston) office of Ginn & Co., successors to Ginn, Heath & Co., and still retains the position. His published literary work has been confined to the catalogues and circulars of Ginn & Co., which in 1885–6 amounted each year to two large volumes. He is a member of the Boston Art Club, a Mugwump, a Congregationalist, and unmarried. His residence is at 29 Beacon St., and office as given above.

WILLIAM LANG SUTHERLAND,
Medford, Minn.

Remained at home, in Bath, N. H., in ill health till the spring of 1878. Having been licensed to preach by the Orange Association, May 7, 1878, he went to Minnesota the next month in the employ of the American Home Missionary Society, and was stationed at Morristown, in that state, till the fall of 1880, having charge of churches there and at Waterville. Then for several months he was engaged in a general missionary work in Big Stone and Traverse counties, being ordained to the Congregational ministry at Ortonville, Minn., Dec. 15, 1880. For one year from April 1, 1881, he was acting pastor of the church at Fergus Falls, Minn.; but his health became badly broken, and he was forced to give up professional work. From July 1882 to Dec. 1883 he was in the employ of E. J. Woodham, furniture dealer and manufacturer, at Fergus Falls, preaching in various places on Sundays as health permitted. At the expiration of this time his health became sufficiently restored to enable him to feel justified in accepting a call to the Congregational church at Medford, Minn., where he still remains. Is an Independent in politics. Was married at Morristown, Minn., Oct. 19, 1880, to Hollie, daughter of Joseph Hopkins of Morristown. Mary Alice was born Sept. 2, 1885, and Anna Waters, May 19, 1887.

WILLIAM FRANKLIN TEMPLE,
316 Shawmut Ave., Boston, Mass.

Spent the first three years after graduation as a student in Harvard Medical School, but did not receive his medical degree until 1881, as he served in the Boston City Hospital from July 1, 1880, till Jan. 1, 1882, retiring as house physician. The time from the last date till the first of August following he spent in travel through Western Europe, going as far south as Sicily, and as far north as Denmark. Since September 1882 he has been in practice in Boston. In 1883 was appointed visiting physician to the St. Elizabeth Hospital, in 1885 district physician to the Boston Dispensary, and in 1886 physician to out-patients at the Carney Hospital. Is a Blue Lodge Mason, member of several benefit societies, and a fellow of the Massachusetts Medical Society. A Mugwump and a Unitarian. Was married in Boston, Sept. 30, 1886, to Mary Alice, daughter of John Ferrin.

SAMUEL BRACKETT THOMBS,
Knightville, Me.

Began the study of medicine in Aug. 1877 at the Portland School for Medical Instruction, teaching a part of the time at Westbrook Seminary, Stevens Plains, Me. Attended two courses of lectures at the Medical School of Maine, at Brunswick, and graduated there in June 1880. After a short rest at home, he located in August at Knightville, Cape Elizabeth, Me., where he has since remained. Has held no office save the chairmanship of the present local board of health. Is a member of the Maine Medical Association, and of the Cumberland County Medical Association; also of Hiram Lodge of Master Masons, Greenleaf Chapter Royal Arch Masons, and St. Alban Commandery Knights Templars. Is a Democrat and a Universalist. Was married at

Lewiston, Me., Aug. 16, 1881, to Ida Asenath, daughter of Josiah Dunn of Lewiston. She died March 2, 1883, and he was again married, Dec. 15, 1884, to Mattie M., daughter of W. B. Nutter of Scarboro', Me. No children.

WILLIAM RIPLEY TILLOTSON,
Moorhead, Minn.

Studied law at Hanover, in the office of Hon. Frederick Chase [D. C. 1860] for three years beginning Sept. 1877, and was admitted to the New Hampshire bar on examination, at Concord, Sept. 2, 1880. Staid in Hanover till the next spring, when he started out to seek his fortune, and in the latter part of March, 1881, landed in Moorhead, Minn., where he has since remained. Was a clerk in the law office of Burnham [D. C. 1869] & Gould until Jan. 1, 1883, when the law firm of Burnham, Mills & Tillotson was formed. This firm existed till Jan. 1, 1887, when Mr. Mills left it to go upon the bench, and the present firm name is Burnham & Tillotson. He was appointed, Dec. 29, 1886, U. S. Commissioner for the District of Minnesota, which is his only office of a political nature. His only publications are various briefs to be found in the volumes of the Minnesota Reports. Is a member of the Knights of Pythias, has filled the highest office in the local lodge, and was a representative to the Grand Lodge, Jurisdiction of Minnesota, in Sept. 1886. In politics a Republican, and an Episcopalian in religious preference. *At present*, he is unmarried.

EDGAR ANDES TWITCHELL,
Pence Opera House, Minneapolis, Minn.

For two years from August 1877 he was a law student in the office of Ray, Drew [D. C. 1870] & Jordan, at Lancaster, N. H. In the fall of 1879 he removed to the office of Geo. W. Cahoon [D. C. 1853], at Lyndon, Vt., and was admitted to the Caledonia county bar, Dec. 9, 1879. In April 1880 he migrated to Albert Lea, Minn., and opened a law office there May 1, continuing in practice till Jan. 1882. From March 20, 1882, to July of the same year he was a member of the firm of Twitchell

& Brown [D. C. 1876], in the real estate commission business, in Minneapolis, and subsequently in the same business either alone or in the firm of Twitchell & Roby till Dec. 3, 1883. At that date he abandoned the commission business, and has since been very successfully engaged in real estate business with his own capital. Has hitherto acted with the Republican party, but has of late been somewhat shaken in his allegiance by his sympathies with the labor and temperance movements. His religious views are skeptical. Was married at Lancaster, N. H., July 26, 1879, to Clara Hall, daughter of Dennis Stanley of Lancaster. Has one child, Stanley Andes, born June 25, 1884.

HERBERT HART WALKER,
99 Nassau St., New York, N. Y.

Taught some time at Chester, Mass. In the fall of 1878 was teaching in the Mt. Washington Institute, New York city. Was for some time teacher of languages in the Selleck School, Norwalk, Ct., and in the fall of 1880 was reported as a teacher at College Point, N. Y. Meanwhile had been studying law in the office of Rufus F. Andrews, New York city, and in 1881 taught in the House of Refuge, in the city, while continuing his law studies. Was admitted to the bar in the fall of 1882, and has since practiced in New York, for a time in the firm of Andrews, Walker & Andrews, but of late alone. A Republican in politics. " Religious preferences the same as when in college." Unmarried.

ALBERT WALLACE,
Rochester, N. H.

Has been since graduation in the employ of E. G. & E. Wallace, manufacturers of leather, boots, and shoes, at Rochester; the first three years worked at the bench, then in the office a few years, and now has charge of one of the two shops devoted to shoe manufacturing. Is also treasurer of the Rochester Aqueduct and Water Co. Is a member of the Humane Lodge, Master Masons, and of Temple Chapter, Royal Arch Masons. In politics a Republican, and in religion inclined to Universalism. Was married, May 23, 1883, to Rosalie Kimball, daughter of Martin L. Burr of Rochester. No children.

SUMNER WALLACE,
Rochester, N. H..

After graduation he worked for about three months in the Rochester Savings Bank, and since has been in the shoe and leather business with E. G. & E. Wallace, except for about a year ending in July 1883, when he was engaged in the manufacture of boots and shoes in the firm of Duntley & Wallace. Was elected supervisor of registration in 1878, and was a member of the Legislature of 1885. Chosen president of the Rochester Loan and Banking Co. in August 1886, and one of the trustees of Rochester Savings Bank in Sept. 1886. Is a Chapter Mason, and an Odd Fellow, in the latter organization having been through the principal chairs. Has always been a Republican, and is strongly inclined to the Universalist faith. Was married, Jan. 30, 1885, at Farmington, N. H., to Harriet Zerega, daughter of Ellison O. Curtis of Farmington. A son, Scott, was born July 12, 1886.

CHARLES ANDREW WILLARD,
63 Loan and Trust Co.'s Building, Minneapolis, Minn.

Studied law with A. E. Rankin, St. Johnsbury, Vt., from July 4, 1877, and was admitted to the bar of Caledonia county, July 2, 1878. Was a member of Boston University School of Law for one year, graduating there in June 1879. He practiced at St. Johnsbury to Jan. 1, 1881, serving also as clerk to the Commissioners on the Revision of the Laws of Vermont from Feb. to June, 1880. Was then librarian of the St. Johnsbury Athenæum from Jan. 1, 1881, to April 1, 1882, and then entered upon legal practice in St. Paul, Minn., in partnership with Willis, under the firm name of Willis & Willard. The firm was dissolved Oct. 1, 1884, and from that date till April 1, 1885, he has practiced alone in St. Paul. Since the last date he has been a member of the law firm of Gilfillan, Belden & Willard, in Minneapolis. Republican ; Episcopalian ; unmarried.

JOHN WILLEY WILLIS,
National German American Bank Building, St. Paul, Minn.

Read law from graduation in the office of Gilman & Clough, in St. Paul, and also taught Latin in the city High School for the school year 1878–9. Was admitted to the Minnesota bar Oct. 18, 1879, and has since been in active practice in St. Paul. Was in partnership with Willard from April 1, 1882, to Oct. 1, 1884, but otherwise has been alone. Is a member of the city Board of Education. Is actively engaged in politics from a Democratic standpoint, has been a member of the State Central Committee, and was the nominee of the party for the office of Attorney General of the state at the election of 1883. Is a communicant of the Protestant Episcopal church. Was married, May 18, 1882, to Eleanor R. Forsyth of St. Paul. They have no children.

JOHN COOPER WINSLOW,

Pasadena, Cal.

Read law in his father's office, at Watertown, N. Y., from graduation, and was admitted to the bar May 1, 1879. Entered into partnership with his father on the 17th of that month, and there remained until his appointment, Jan. 1, 1880, to the head clerkship in the office of the Attorney General of New York, at Albany. Was visited with a severe lung trouble in the early winter of 1882–3, and spent the latter part of the winter in Florida. Returned the first of May, and resumed work at Albany, being obliged to give up again, however, the last of June. He went at once into the Adirondack region, and remained there for some time, with apparent good results. Afterwards made trial of Mexico and New Mexico as a health resort, and some two years since located in the practice of law at Pasadena, Cal., well known for its delightful climate. Have not heard from him for a year past, and do not know the present condition of his health. Was married, May 13, 1880, to Isabel Bates of Syracuse, N. Y. They have no children.

NON-GRADUATES.

WILLIAM SILAS BAILEY,

East Hardwick, Vt.

Left the class at the close of our freshman year, and soon after entered Williams College, where he was connected with the class of '78. Left during his senior year, and did not graduate. Was for some time employed as clerk in a furniture establishment at East Cambridge, Mass., and in 1882 was reported as a commission merchant in Boston, in the firm of Williams, Bailey & Co. Has been at East Hardwick, Vt., since the spring of 1886, in charge of a stock farm, raising blooded horses. Was married, Oct. 10, 1882, to F. M. Martin of Peacham, Vt. A newspaper item gives the birth of a daughter, Feb. 7, 1887; whether there are other children is unknown to the Secretary.

WOOSTER ORLIN BALL,
Watertown, N. Y.

Left the class at the close of sophomore year. For one year was in his father's employ, engaged in buying produce, and since that time, till Jan. 12, 1887, was in partnership with him in the general produce business, under the firm name of H. M. Ball & Son. Since the last date he has been in the hardware business, as junior member of the firm of W. W. Conde & Co. Since Oct. 1, 1884, has also been interested in the manufacture of carriage gearing and carriage wood-work, as secretary and treasurer of the Maud S. Gear Company. Was married, June 23, 1881, to Kate L., daughter of George Baker of Chicago, Ill. They have one daughter, born Nov. 2, 1886.

JOHN JAMES BERRY,
Portsmouth, N. H.

Left college sophomore fall. Spent the year 1876–7 in Harvard Medical School, and then completed his medical studies at the University of New York, where he graduated Feb. 19, 1878. From October 1877 to October 1878 he was a student and assistant of Dr. G. W. Howe, visiting surgeon to Charity Hospital, Blackwell's Island, and to St. Francis' Hospital, New York city. From Oct. 1, 1878, to April 1, 1879, he was assistant surgeon in the New York Hospital, House of Relief; from the last date till May 26, 1879, in St. Francis' Hospital, and then in the Hospital for the Ruptured and Crippled till April 1, 1881. He then spent several months in European travel. Opened practice at Fall River, Mass., in October 1881, and remained there about eight months. In 1882 located at South Norwalk, Ct., and in 1885 removed to Portsmouth, N. H., his present location. Member of New Hampshire Medical Society, American Public Health Association, American Medical Association, one of the secretaries in the Section of Anatomy of the International Medical Congress, which meets in Washington, D. C., in September 1887, and president of the Portsmouth Medical Association. Has contributed various articles on surgical and anatomical subjects to the *Medical Record, New England Medical Monthly, Annals of Anatomy and Surgery, Medical Register, Maryland Medical Journal,* and *Boston Medical and Surgical Journal.* Is the author of an article on "Diseases of the Joints," printed in the *Transactions of the Connecticut Medical Society,* and of two leading articles for the *Medical History of Connecticut,* now in press. An essay entitled, *How can the Mortality of Consumption be reduced,* read before a sanitary convention in Manchester, N. H., Jan. 26, 1887, has been printed in pamphlet form (pp. 15). Is an attendant at an Episcopal church. Has no politics to report. Was married, Oct. 26, 1881, to Fannie Emily, daughter of George Craus of New York city. They have one daughter, Ida Marguerite, born Aug. 13, 1882.

Francis Beattie Brewer, Jr.,
Ottawa Station, Mich.

Left the class at the end of freshman year and entered Yale College. After one term there he left on account of ill health. In the spring of 1875 he was employed for a few months in a wholesale hardware store in Chicago. From the fall of 1875 till the summer of 1877 he was connected with the *Erie Morning Dispatch,* Erie, Pa., and from November 1877 to January 1878 was in the employ of the Erie Publishing Co. At the last date became a member of the firm of Allen & Brewer, book-sellers, at Erie. In April 1880 bought out his partner's share of the business, and conducted it alone till April 1882. Since 1882 has been most of the time in Michigan, engaged in reclaiming and improving some wild land, of which he has about 5,000 acres for sale, and expects to remain there. Is a Republican and a Methodist; unmarried.

WILBUR FRANKLIN BRYANT,

West Point, Cuming Co., Neb.

Left the class at the close of freshman year, and read law at Lebanon, N. H., in the office of John L. Spring, from Dec. 6, 1874, to Aug. 29, 1876. Then he went to Green Island, Neb., and taught there five months through the winter of 1876-7. Having finished his law studies with John R. Gamble of Yankton, Dak., he was admitted to the bar April 17, 1877, and practiced there a few weeks. From June 1877 to Jan. 23, 1884, he practiced at St. Helena, Neb., and from the last date to the next December at Aten, Neb. Since this time he has been located at West Point, Neb. In 1877 was chosen Justice of the Peace, but refused to qualify; in 1878 declined an appointment as county judge for Cedar county; was county attorney for some time from Nov. 1879; was commissioned postmaster at St. Helena, April 27, 1881, and held the office for three years; in Nov. 1882 was elected District Attorney for the Sixth District of Nebraska, including the whole northern portion of the state, from Wyoming to Iowa, the term being from Jan. 1, 1883, to Jan. 1, 1885; in Nov. 1885 was elected Judge of the County Court of Cuming county, and entered upon the duties of the office Jan. 7, 1886. A political speech of his has been issued in pamphlet form, and he is the author of a book entitled *The Blood of Abel* (copyright, 1887, pp. 169), which is a review of the conduct of President Cleveland and Secretary Bayard in the affair of Louis Riel; has also contributed two articles to the *Bible Examiner*, entitled, *The Scripture Unscathed.* Is a member of the Catholic Knights of America, a Republican, and a member of the Roman Catholic Church. Was married, at Springfield, Dak., Oct. 1, 1881, to Katy, daughter of Stephen P. Saunders. They have two daughters, Ita, born June 16, 1884, and Ethel, born May 5, 1886.

ADDISON EDWARD CUDWORTH,

South Londonderry, Vt.

Left the class at the end of the first term of sophomore year. Taught in the spring of 1875 at Bradford, N. H., and in the ensuing fall and winter at Marlow, N. H. He then re-entered college in the class of '78, remaining with them, however, only till the end of the year. Taught at Weston, Vt., in the winter of 1876–7, and then began the study of law with James L. Martin, at South Londonderry, Vt. Taught at Mechanicsville, Vt., in the winter of 1877–8. Was admitted to the Windham county bar, at Newfane, Vt., Sept. 12, 1879, and has since practiced at South Londonderry, being for a time in partnership with Hon. J. L. Martin, and since alone. Represented the town in the Legislature of 1884, serving on the Committee on Education. A Republican in politics. Was married, April 15, 1880, to Mary E. Rogers of West Hebron, N. Y. Their children are Clyde Earl, born Feb. 6, 1881, and Ina Sara, born June 19, 1882.

WILLIAM HENRY CUMMINGS,

Thetford, Vt.

Left the class in the fall of sophomore year, and then taught at Chelsea, Vt., till the spring of 1876. In the following fall he returned to college and entered the class of '79, with which class he graduated. Was then for five years principal of Bradford (Vt.) Academy, and since of Thetford Academy. In politics, he is a Republican, with Prohibitory leanings. Is a member of the Congregational church at Thetford, and was deacon of the church at Bradford during the last few months of his residence there. Was married, Nov. 25, 1879, to Julia Vincent, daughter of Alonzo H. Powers of Chelsea, Vt. Julia Victoria, born April 26, 1881, received the class cup of '79; a twin daughter lived but two days.

WILLIAM ADAMS DRESSER,

330 Robert St., St. Paul, Minn.

At the close of freshman year transferred his relations to Amherst College, where he graduated with the class of '77. Was for some months at his home at Castine, Me., occupied with teaching private pupils, and from March 1878 to the close of the school year was teacher of languages in the State Normal School at Castine. At this time his health gave way, and he went abroad in the summer of '78, remaining three years. Spent most of the time in Italy, France, Switzerland, and Austria, steadily regaining health, and studying languages, literature, and art. Spent the first year after returning from Europe in business with his father, at Castine, but found the New England climate unfavorable, and went to St. Paul, Minn., in the fall of '82. Was occupied for the following three years with teaching French, Italian, Greek, and Latin, and with real estate investments. From the fall of '85 to August 1886 was a partner in a decorating and furnishing house, and since that date has been in his present business of investment securities, mortgages, and real estate. Declined an offer, last December, of the chair of Modern Languages in MacAlester College, St. Paul. In politics is a very independent Republican; a member of a Congregational church. "Neither married nor have any expectation in that direction."

BRAYTON ALLEN FIELD,

Watertown, N. Y.

Left the class at the end of sophomore year from ill health, and for the next year and two-thirds was engaged in recruiting. Taught at home (East Hounsfield, N. Y.) in the winter of 1876–7, and in the spring of '77 returned to college, entering the class of '78, and graduated with that class. Was then for one year principal of Proctor Academy, Andover, N. H. In Aug. 1879 entered the law office of O'Brien & Emerson, Watertown, N. Y. Was also for the year 1879–80 principal of one of the city grammar schools, continuing his law studies meanwhile. In June 1880 his health had become so broken down that he was obliged to give up study and teaching, and spent the next three years on his father's farm. In Dec. 1883 he resumed his law studies in the same office with regained health, and was admitted to the bar of New York, at Utica, April 21, 1886. Remained with the same firm till December, and then, on its dissolution, opened an office with E. C. Emerson, the former junior partner. Is a Republican, and a member of a Christian church. Was married, April 27, 1881, to Nettie Elizabeth, daughter of Judge William C. Thompson of Watertown. Their children are Nellie Louise, born Dec. 8, 1884, and Allan Thompson, born June 18, 1886.

HEMAN ALLEN HALSTED,

Hamburgh, N. J.

Left the class freshman fall, and in the fall of 1874 returned, entering the class of '78, but remained only a few weeks. Taught for the rest of the year at Windham, N. J. Subsequently read law in New York city, in the office of C. & N. D. Lawton, and later with C. A. Runk. From 1879 to 1881 he was principal of the Deckertown, N. J., Public Schools, and was then for a time traveling agent for the Union Publishing House of New York. From 1882 to 1884 he practiced law at Deckertown, N. J., and since at Hamburgh, N. J. Is president of the Eureka Lodge of Knights and Ladies of the Golden Star. In politics a Republican. A communicant of the Protestant Episcopal church, and a lay reader of the diocese of Newark. Was married, Dec. 26, 1883, to Sarah Frances, daughter of John B. Thompson of Deckertown. Their children are: Ernest Allen, born Oct. 4, 1884; Tracy Lee, born March 16, 1886; May, born May 20, 1887.

CHARLES HENRY WEBSTER HOWE, son of Benjamin Darwin and Eliza (Hitchcock) Howe, was born at Hanover, N. H., June 24, 1856. His father was a bookbinder, and died at Hanover in 1867. He fitted for college at Norwich Academy, and left the class in the winter of sophomore year, from ill health. His health having considerably improved, in the fall of 1876 he resumed his studies in the class of '78, and graduated with that class. He then engaged in the study of medicine at Hanover, and would have taken his degree in June 1881. The last years of his life were a continual struggle with consumption, and he failed rapidly after an attack of acute bronchitis, in December 1880. In the February following he was taken to Aiken, S. C., but lost strength continually while there, and remained but four weeks Returning from the South, he went no farther than New York, where the last three weeks of his life were passed, at the Fifth Avenue Hotel, and where he died on the night of April 25, 1881. The funeral services were held at Hanover on the 29th, and his body lies buried in the familiar cemetery there. He was a member of the College church, and his death is said to have been unusually happy and peaceful.

Louis Gilman Hoyt,
Kingston, N. H.

Left the class freshman spring, and the next fall taught at
Osterville, Mass.   Read law at Exeter, N. H., with W. W. Stick-
ney [D. C. 1823], and was admitted to the bar Jan. 14, 1878.
Remained at Exeter till the May following, when he opened an
office at Kingston, N. H., where he has since remained.   Has
not been heard from of late.   Was unmarried at last accounts.

John Hall Ives,
206 Broadway, New York, N. Y.

He left the class during the spring of freshman year, and is
said to have been engaged in stenography for a time.   One brief
note in 1881 comprises the extent of his communications to the
Secretary.   At that time he was practicing law in New York
city, and is understood to be still in the same place and occupa-
tion.

James Davidson Maxwell, son of John and Elizabeth
(Davidson) Maxwell, was born at Cohoes, N. Y., Sept. 3, 1851.
His parents were natives of Scotland, and his home from early
youth was at Amsterdam, N. Y., where his father was engaged
in manufacturing.   In 1870 he entered Cornell University, and
remained there about two years, in a scientific course.   He left
Dartmouth before the end of our first term, and went into business with his father.   In 1877 he engaged in the manufacture of
hosiery with his brother, at Amsterdam, and was thereafter so
engaged.   He twice visited Europe, once in 1877, and again in
1880, on his bridal tour.   He was married, Sept. 1, 1880, to Hattie H., daughter of Charles M. Morrell of Amsterdam, and a
daughter was born to them Nov. 1, 1881.   While on his way
home from New York city, Nov. 12, 1882, he was injured by a
railway collision at Peekskill, N. Y., and died at Peekskill on
the 27th of that month, after intense and protracted suffering.
Maxwell First was with us but a short time, but our associations
with him were of the pleasantest, and he is sure of an abiding
place in our memory.

WILLIAM GRAY MAXWELL,
Amsterdam, N. Y.

Left the class during the first term of freshman year, and went into hosiery manufacturing at Amsterdam.   While engaged in business he devoted some time to the study of law, spending the year 1876–7 in Harvard Law School.   Spent some months in European travel in 1877, and again in 1880.   In 1885 he retired from manufacturing, the firm at that time employing some three hundred hands, and turning out over $50,000 worth of goods yearly.   He then went into the practice of law in partnership with an older brother in New York city, residing at Yonkers.   They have lately removed their office to Amsterdam, but expect to return to New York for a permanent location. Several articles from his pen, chiefly on economical or philosophical subjects, have been published in monthly magazines.   In connection with his brother, he published, in 1886, a law book in popular form entitled *The Rights and Obligations of Marriage.* Is a Republican ; without religious preference ; unmarried.

WINFIELD SCOTT MONTGOMERY,
1912 Eleventh St., N. W., Washington, D. C.

Left the class at the close of sophomore year, taught for a year in Washington, D. C., and then returned to college, graduating with the class of '78.   Taught a Graded School at Anacostia, D. C., in the fall of 1878, and then from Dec. 1878 till 1882 was Professor of Ancient Languages in Alcorn University, Rodney, Miss.   Since 1882 he has been one of the supervising principals of the public schools of the District of Columbia.   Is one of the vice-presidents of the American Institute of Instruction for the present year.   Is a Republican in politics, and a member of a Baptist church.   Was married at Columbia, S. C., Aug. 9, 1883, to Emma Rosa, daughter of Charles M. Wilder of Columbia.   Wilder Percival was born May 26, 1884, and Marcia, April 13, 1887.

WILLIAM HENRY MOORE,
Portsmouth, N. H.

Left college at the Thanksgiving recess, freshman fall, and taught in the following winter.   Was employed as a clerk the greater part of the year 1874. In 1875 returned to Portsmouth, and began the study of law with James D. Butler, so continuing until Dec. 16, 1875, when he entered the U. S. Navy, as a yeoman on board the U. S. S. Marion. Sailed from Portsmouth, Jan. 24, 1876, and after six months in the North Atlantic and the Gulf of Mexico, proceeded to the Mediterranean, and was discharged at his own request, Jan. 7, 1877, at Ville Franche sur Mer, in Southeastern France. Then made a trip through France and England, and in the latter part of July, at Liverpool, shipped on board the bark Memory, for Balize, British Honduras, returning to Liverpool in November. Thence went to Glasgow, and there, in February 1878, shipped on board the American bark Devonshire for Buenos Ayres. Arrived at the latter city in April, and proceeded down the coast of Patagonia for a load of guano under papers issued by the Argentine Republic. While taking in guano at an island claimed both by the Argentine Republic and Chili, a Chilian cruiser in October seized the bark as a prize, and took her to Punta Arenas, in the Straits of Magellan. At that place he left the bark, and remained there in various occupations till January 1880, when he shipped on board the British schooner Felis, and went to the Falkland Islands. There, in June 1880, he shipped once more on board the U. S. S. Marion, this time as schoolmaster, the steamer then being assigned to the South Atlantic station In February 1882 was appointed apothecary, and on the return of the steamer to Portsmouth, Dec. 6, 1882, he left the service, and has remained at that place ever since. Studied medicine for a time and did considerable private tutoring. In July 1885 became local editor of the *Portsmouth Journal*, and since July 1886 has been a member of the regular editorial staff of that paper. Has also been for some time engaged in insurance business, and since July 1886 has been of the firm of Ilsley & Moore, fire, life, and accident insurance agents and brokers. Is an Independent Republican, "but no Mugwump." In religion is "thoroughly liberal, and inclined to be agnostic." Was married, Jan. 5, 1887, to Arabel B., daughter of the late James W. Bowles of Portsmouth.

Albert Hayes Morton,
6 Mulberry St., Providence, R. I.

Left college at the end of junior year, and from July 31, 1876, to February 1879 worked as machinist in the machine shop of the Salmon Falls Manufacturing Co., at Salmon Falls, N. H. Then went to Harrisburg, Texas, and worked in the same capacity in the shops of the Galveston, Harrisburg & San Antonio R. R. Left there in May 1879, and went to Milwaukee, Wis., and engaged with E. P. Allis & Co., but in response to a telegram returned to Salmon Falls to take charge of building new machinery for the Salmon Falls Manufacturing Co., and worked there as machinist from June 1879 to Jan. 1, 1880. At that date was appointed master mechanic, and remained there in that capacity till Feb. 28, 1883. From March 1, 1883, to May 1886, he was at Lowell, Mass., in the employ of the Whitehead & Atherton Machine Co., as head draughtsman. Since May 26, 1886, he has been draughtsman for the Brown & Sharpe Manufacturing Co., Providence, R. I., being their leading designer of machinery. Is a Mason, and has held the offices of J. W., S. W., and J. D. A Republican in politics, and in religion an Agnostic. Was married, Feb. 14, 1881, to Jessie F., daughter of E. S. Nowell of Salmon Falls. They have one child, Albert Nowell, born March 9, 1882.

Edward Arthur Murdock,
Spencer, Mass.

Left college at the close of sophomore year, and spent the next three years in the Boston University School of Medicine, from which he graduated March 6, 1878. He practiced at Watertown, Mass., from April 1, 1878, to March 1, 1883, and since the last date at Spencer, Mass. Is a member of the Massachusetts, Worcester County, and Western Massachusetts Homeopathic Medical Societies, having been Vice-President of the second; also of the Royal Arcanum (medical examiner), American Legion of Honor, Home Circle, and Golden Rule Alliance (medical examiner). Is a Republican, and a member of a Congregational church. Was married at Groton, Mass., July 24, 1879, to Mary P., daughter of W. C. Turner of Groton. Their children are Susie Mary, born Jan. 18, 1881, and Arthur Edward, born Feb. 5, 1885.

FRANK WILLIAM PATTEN,
Hopkinton, Mass.

Left college at the end of freshman year, and in the fall ensuing began the study of medicine with Dr. W. W. Wilkins of Manchester, N. H. Attended lectures at the College of Physicians and Surgeons, New York, during the sessions of 1875–6 and 1876–7, graduating there March 1, 1877. After spending some time there in special study, he returned to Manchester, and remained in the office of Dr. Thomas Wheat through the summer. In Oct. 1877 he settled in practice at Hopkinton, Mass., where he still remains. Was school committee in 1882 and '3, and health officer three years. Is a member of the Free Masons, Knights of Honor, and the Thurber Medical Society, and has held various offices in each. Is a Republican, and a member and treasurer of the First Congregational church of Hopkinton. Was married, Sept. 20, 1876, to Harriette Elizabeth, daughter of William Bailey of Manchester. Their children are: William Everett, born Aug. 16, 1877 ; Arthur Howard, born March 17, 1879 ; Clarence Wesley, born March 8, 1881 ; Bertha Alice, born July 24, 1884.

ROBERT ALLEN RAY,
Concord, N. H.

Left college at the end of freshman year, and taught the High School at Townsend, Mass., during the next year. In the spring of 1875 he began the study of law at Concord in the office of Sargent [D. C. 1840] & Chase [C. S. D. 1858], and was admitted to the New Hampshire bar April 23, 1878. Meanwhile he taught as assistant in the Concord High School from Sept. 1876 to Sept. 1878. In Sept. 1878 he began practice at Concord in the firm of Ray & Walker, and so remains. Has been at work for two years on Ray & Walker's Book of New Hampshire Citations, under a contract with the state of New Hampshire. Was elected city solicitor, Nov. 1880, and held the office by re-elections till Feb. 1885. Was a member of the Legislature from Ward 6, Concord, in 1885, and served·on the Com-

mittee on Railroads.   In April 1887 was appointed by Gov. Currier Associate Justice of the Police Court of Concord.   Is a Republican, and a member of a Baptist church   Was married, Jan.
18, 1881, to H. Annie, daughter of Oliver Ballou of Concord.
A daughter, Agnes H., was born March 18, 1883.

WILLIAM HENRY RAY,

Corner 57th St. and Monroe Ave., Chicago, Ill.

Left the class at the end of junior year, and after acting as
principal of the Norwich (Vt.) Academy for one year, returned to
college, and took his senior year and graduated with '78.   From
Sept. 1878 till Jan. 1881 he was principal of McCollom Institute,
Mt. Vernon, N. H.; from Jan. to July, 1881, sub-master of Grammar School No. 2, Yonkers, N. Y.; from July 1881 to July 1883
superintendent of schools at Waukegan, Ill.; and since July
1883 principal of the Hyde Park High School, within the city
of Chicago.   Since 1882 he has also served by appointment of
the State Superintendent as one of the institute conductors of
the state.   For one year (1880–1) he was town superintendent
at Mt. Vernon.   An article entitled *Russia in Asia*, in the *Atlantic Monthly* for March 1887, is from his pen; has also been a frequent contributor to professional periodicals, and the author of
occasional lectures.   Is a member of the Illinois State Teachers' Association (its first Vice-President for 1885), Society of
Illinois Principals (chairman of the Executive Committee for
1885–6), Northern Illinois Teachers' Association (Secretary for
1884–6), Society of High School Teachers of Illinois (Vice-President for 1886–7), Chicago Institute of Education, Northwestern
Association of High School Teachers (President for 1887–8),
and also of the Chicago Literary Club; is also Secretary of the
National Educational Exposition, held in Chicago, July 1887, in
connection with the National Educational Association.   Usually
acts with the Republican party.   Is a member of the Frst Presbyterian church of Hyde Park, member of its music committee
and assistant superintendent of its Sunday-School.   Was married at Norwich, Vt., June 12, 1880, to Martha Hunt, daughter
of Henry Hutchinson of Norwich.   A son, Duncan, was born
April 17, 1884, and died Aug. 30, 1885.

FRANK SUMNER ROGERS,
Troy, Vt.

Left the class at the close of sophomore year, and returned to college in the spring of 1877, entering the class of '78, with which class he graduated. In the fall of 1878 he taught at Troy, Vt., and then began the study of law at that place, in the office of H. E. Powell, continuing it later with P. M. Gleed of Morrisville, Vt. Is now practicing at Troy, and is believed to have been there most, if not all, the time since his admission to the bar. He is never induced to report. Was married at Troy, April 11, 1882, to Alice Aiken of Jay, Vt., and is said to have three children.

ALBERT PARKER SANBORN, son of David and Mary Jane (Smith) Sanborn, was born at Lake Village, N. H., Nov. 17, 1855. His father was a molder in an iron foundry. He fitted for college at the New Hampshire Conference Seminary, at Tilton. He left college at the end of the first term of sophomore year on account of ill health, and died at his home at Lake Village, Aug. 20, 1876, just before the re-assembling of the class at the beginning of senior year. Atkinson was present at the funeral. Sanborn was a member of the Free Baptist church at Lake Village. This death was the only one occurring in the class during our college course.

EDWIN WEBSTER SANBORN,
32 Nassau St., New York, N. Y.

Left the class at the end of sophomore year, and after a year's absence from college entered the class of '78, with which class he graduated. Studied law at Columbia Law School and in the office of Rufus F. Andrews, New York, one year, and was then for two years teacher of Latin and Greek in the High School of St. Paul, Minn. In the fall of 1881 he resumed his law studies in New York, was admitted to the bar in January 1882, and soon after opened an office there. Since May 1, 1884, has been a member of the law firm of Clark & Sanborn, at the above address.   Politically, he is a Mugwump.   As yet unmarried.

ISAAC S SCHULTZ,

Miles City, Montana.

Left college in November of sophomore year on account of ill health.   In the following winter he taught four months at Ellaville, Pa., and was then, from April to September, 1875, on his father's farm at Hereford, Pa. From the last date to Feb. 1879 he was engaged in orange growing at Fort Mason, Orange Co., Fla., but did not find the climate suited to his health, and returned to Pennsylvania.   In the winter of 1879–80 he taught the Schultzville school, in Colebrookdale, Pa., and then, in April, engaged in farm work in Kane County, Ill., for the benefit of his health, remaining there till March 1881.   For the next year he taught at Bordeaux, Wyoming, and spent the summer of '82 in Florida, looking after his orange grove, which he had still retained.   Since October 1882 he has been located in Montana, on a sheep ranch.   The Secretary has not heard from him directly for several years, but thinks his address is still as above.

WILLIAM JAMES SHEPARD,

Watertown, N. Y.

Left Dartmouth at the end of sophomore year, and entered Wesleyan University, remaining there but one term.   For a time he studied law at Watertown, N. Y., and was clerk of the Senate Committee on Privileges and Elections, at Albany, during the session of 1878.   From Feb. 18, 1879, till April 1, 1884, he held the office of City Chamberlain of Watertown, receiving five annual elections, but being finally defeated by a political overturn in the city.   Immediately on retiring from this position he became a member of the firm of Ingalls, Shepard & Dewey, publishers of *The Watertown Post*, a weekly newspaper, continuing in this business till Jan. 19, 1886.   For about six months ending with Jan. 1886 the firm also published a daily, the *Watertown Daily Republican*.   For some time following he was in the employ of a New York firm in the preparation of a county atlas. Since Feb. 1, 1887, he has been employed as special agent of the Watertown Steam Engine Co., this position promising to be

permanent. Is a member of the city police commission for four
years from May 1, 1885. Is an Odd Fellow, having filled all
the chairs in the subordinate lodge, and having been trustee and
proxy delegate to the grand lodge. A Republican in politics,
and a communicant of the Protestant Episcopal church. Was
married, Feb. 13, 1884, to Lydia Margaret, daughter of Azariah
Nellis of Watertown. Frieda Margaret was born Sept. 6, 1885,
and died Sept. 11, 1885; Helen Josephine was born Sept. 2,
1886.

WARRINGTON SOMERS,

Auburn, N. Y.

Left college sophomore fall, and taught during the following winter at Peacham, Vt. For one year from the fall of 1875
he was principal of the High School at Warrensburg, N. Y., and
of the Union School at Greenwich, N. Y., from 1876 to 1882.
He was then teaching for a short time at Wellsville, N. Y., and
has been for the last four years and a half assistant principal of
the High School at Auburn, N. Y. He received the honorary
degree of Master of Arts in 1877 from some college in the state
of New York. Was married, Feb. 19, 1875, to Mary A., daughter of Rev. Leviny H. Hooker of Peacham, Vt. Is said to have
a number of children. Has never made a direct report, and the
above information has been obtained from other sources.

MARTIN LUTHER STIMSON,

Tientsin, China.

Left the class at the end of sophomore year, and after a
year's absence entered the class of '78, with which class he
graduated. He then spent three years in Oberlin Theological
Seminary, graduating there in June 1881. Having been accepted for missionary service by the American Board, he was ordained at Oberlin, and assigned to a new mission in the prov-
ince of Shanse, China. Sailed from San Francisco, Sept. 6,
1881, and arrived at Fungchow, near Peking, Oct. 21. In June
following, he proceeded to his mission field, arriving at T'ai Yuan
Fu July 4. Removed in October 1883 to Chieh Hsiee Hsien,
in April 1884 to T'aiku Hsien, and in December 1886 to Fêu
Chow Fu, where he now remains, the post-office address of the

mission, however, being as above. Has been secretary of the mission from its organization, and treasurer for the last year. In politics would call himself a Prohibitionist, and in religion a Congregationalist—"stiff, old-fashioned New England orthodox." Was married at Oberlin, O., July 6, 1881, to Emily Brooks, daughter of Rev. Heman B. Hall, the lady being a graduate of Oberlin in 1881. Their children are as follows: Leonard Martin, born April 15, 1882, died Feb. 14, 1884; James Palmer Stone, born July 5, 1883; Edith May, born April 1, 1886.

JOHN QUINCY STONE,
Northampton, Mass.

Left college freshman winter, and taught that winter at Groton, Mass. From September 1874 to June 1875 he studied medicine with Dr. Norman Smith of Groton, from the latter date to the following December canvassed for the *Boston Cultivator*, and then taught at Shirley, Mass., till March 1876. From May to July of that year he made collections for the *Boston Cultivator*, and from December 1876 to March 1877 he taught at Charlton, Mass. From March 11, 1877, to April 19, 1879, he was a member of the dental firm of Palmer & Stone, at Ayer, Mass. From the last date to April 1, 1881, he traveled as a dentist through Massachusetts, Connecticut and Vermont, and has since been located in practice at Northampton, Mass. Is a Democrat and a Congregationalist. Was married, Nov. 20, 1880, at Harvard, Mass., to Sarah D., daughter of Edward Clapp of Northampton. A daughter, Estella A., was born Oct. 6, 1881.

WARREN STORY,
San Bernardino, Cal.

Left college at the end of our first term, and has made the Secretary no end of trouble. In the spring of '77 he was said to be farming at Dunbarton, N. H., his old home. Afterwards he was for some years in San Francisco, Cal., where he was, for a time at least, a member of the firm of C. James King of William & Co., packers and dealers in hermetically sealed goods. Since February 1882 he has been at San Bernardino, where he appears to have a fruit ranch, and to be largely interested in the prevailing land speculations of that section. In December 1886 the postmaster reported him as engaged in the real estate and abstract business. Is married, and has at least one. child—a daughter, now four years old.

ARTHUR FRENCH TOWNE,
97 Clark St., Chicago, Ill.

Left college freshman fall, and taught that winter at Walpole, N. H. He then read law one year with J. G. Bellows at Walpole, and two years in the Boston University School of Law, graduating there in the spring of 1876. He continued his law studies in Boston, and was admitted to the bar there Oct. 16, 1877. Went at once to Chicago, and has since been in practice there. A Republican in politics. Not married, so far as reported.

CHARLES ARTHUR TUCKER,
Norwalk, Ct.

Left the class freshman fall, returning to college in the fall of 1875 to enter the class of '78, with which class he graduated. Was cashier in a grocery store at Elizabeth, N. J., from August 1878 to January 1879. Was then until the following summer assistant in the public schools of Manchester, Iowa, and then in a similar position at Lansing, Iowa, during the school year 1879–80. For the year 1880–1 he taught Latin in Lenox College, at Hopkinton, Iowa, and since 1881 has been principal of the Center School, at Norwalk, Ct. He is a chronic delinquent in reporting, but it is learned from the '78 class reports that he has been assistant superintendent of the Congregational Sunday-School at Norwalk and president of the Norwalk Literary Society, that he is now organist at the First Baptist church and is a Mason. Was married, Aug. 1, 1883, to Carrie M. Quintard of Norwalk.

HENRY LEWIS WEBB,
Alexandria, Va.

Left college freshman spring, in consequence of breaking his leg while playing foot-ball on the campus. Was then for some months at his home, in Manchester, N. H. From Feb. 1875 to May 1876 he was in the employ of a Boston caterer, and .

then for over a month a waiter at Memorial Hall, Cambridge.
From July to November, 1876, he worked at the Metropolitan
Hotel, Boston.   He started for Virginia, Nov. 30, with the intention of teaching, and located at Alexandria.   From January
to May, 1877, he taught at Stewartsville, Bedford Co., Va., in
the winter of 1881–2 in Fairfax Co., near Alexandria, in the win-
ters of '83–4 and '84–5 at Franconia, Fairfax Co., and the winter of '86–7 at Moorefield, W. Va.   In the summer of '77 worked as waiter at the Pequot Hotel, New London, and at the
Grand Union Hotel, Saratoga Springs, in the summer of '78 and
each summer since, except that of '82, which was spent at the
Prospect House, Shelter Island.   During the time not account-
ed for above, he has been engaged in various kinds of labor in
or near Alexandria.   A Republican in politics.   Member and
clerk of the Alfred St. Baptist church of Alexandria.   Was married, Sept. 19, 1878, to Agnes, daughter of Joseph Smith of Alexandria.   Their children are : Abbie Stark, born Oct. 8, 1878 ;
Agnes Maud, born Aug. 2, 1880; Willie Francis, born Dec. 10,
1882 ; Henry Lewis, Jr., born Nov. 12, 1884.

WILLIAM JOSIAH WILLARD,

Lyndonville, Vt.

Left college sophomore winter from ill health, and soon after became a clerk in the office of the Connecticut and Passumpsic R. R. Co., at Lyndonville, Vt., remaining there till June 1,
1878.   From July 1878 to Dec. 1879 he was station agent for
the same company at St. Johnsbury, and at the last date was
transferred to their general freight office at Lyndonville. Since
Jan. 1, 1883, has been General Freight Agent of the company,
which has now become the Passumpsic Division of the Boston
& Lowell.   Is a Republican in politics, and liberal in religion.
Was married, Nov. 9, 1881, to Martha L., daughter of Charles
Sanborn of Lyndon, Vt.   They have no children.

CHANDLER SCIENTIFIC DEPARTMENT.

ARTHUR HENRY BALDWIN after graduation was employed
in surveying mining claims at Deadwood, Dakota, in 1879 was
assistant engineer of the Homestake Mining Co., at Lead City,
in 1880 Engineer in Chief of the Bed Rock Flume Co. at Deadwood. In 1882 he returned east as far as St. Louis and entered
the employ of the Iron Mountain R. R., of which road he was
assistant engineer in 1883. In 1884 he reported as Assistant
Superintendent of Works in the Mississippi River Improvement
in Engineering Dept. U. S. Army and is now a civil engineer at
Winfield, Kans. Married, January 11, 1882 to Miss Mary Arthur,
daughter of Frederick Arthur of Rockerville, Dak. Address,
Winfield, Kans.

GEORGE WILLIAM BARTLETT has been engaged in railroading ever since graduation, and the following is a good indication
of the success he has met with. September 1877, clerk in local
freight office C. B. & Q. R. R., at Council Bluffs, Iowa ; March
1879, engineer on double track of N. Y., L. E. & W. R. R., Buffalo, N. Y. November 1879, in office of the Division Superintendent of same road, at Port Jervis. N. Y. September 1881,
Supervisor of Track, same road, Narrowsburgh, N. Y. May
1882, Roadmaster same road, at Port Jervis, N. Y. February
1886, Superintendent Rochester Division, same road, at Rochester, N. Y. February 1887, Superintendent Western Division
N. Y., P. & O. R. R., which is leased by the N. Y., L. E. & W.
R. R. Married, June 24, 1883, to Miss Juliette Thomas, daughter
of B. Thomas, Esq., of Port Jervis at the residence of the
bride's uncle, Richard Thomas, Columbus, Ohio. Has two
children, Francis Harris, born at Port Jervis, January 24, 1885,
and Robert Duncan, born at Rochester, Nov. 12, 1886. He is
a Blaine Republican. Address, Rochester, N. Y.

GEORGE FRANKLIN CANIS has devoted himself almost con-
tinuously to journalism since graduation, having been connected

with papers in Baltimore, Md., Boston, Mass., Omaha, Neb., and New York city, besides being editor of the *Las Vegas* (N. M.) *Gazette* and proprietor·of the *News and Press* of Cimarron, and the *News and Press* of Raton, New Mexico. While in the west was engaged in cattle, mining, and land. Postmaster at Deming, N. M., about one year, a member of the Republican Territorial Committee, and Secretary Colfax Co. Republican Committee of New Mexico. Unmarried, Tammany Democrat, and a Ritualist. Address, care of *The World*, Park Row, New York city.

SAMUEL CLARK after graduation was with his brother-in-law at Quechee, Vt., for a while. In the winter of 1877 he went to the Black Hills as a surveyor, and later to Leadville, Colo.; in 1879 was with King's U. S. Geological Survey, and in 1880 book-keeper and assayer of the Adelaide Mining Co., at Leadville, Colo. He had returned to Quechee in January 1881, and in 1882 worked at farming near Denver, Colo.; in 1883 he went to Glendive, Montana, to engage in stock raising, and this year reports himself as still there. Unmarried; Republican; no religious preference. Address, Glendive, Montana.

ARTHUR PRESCOTT FRENCH was principal of the Hancock (N. H.) High School in the fall of 1879, was teaching in Ashuelot, Mass., in 1881–2, and in Marlow Academy, 1882–4. He went to Keene, N. H., May 15, 1884, where he was, I understand, employed in city engineering. He has not reported since 1885, but I have his receipt, dated in August last, for a registered letter at Avon, N. Y., the letter having been forwarded there from Keene.

RAY TIMOTHY GILE entered the Thayer School of Civil Engineering in the fall of 1877, and graduated in June 1879. In the fall of 1879 he was superintendent of a mine in Grafton, N. H.; in the spring of 1880 telephone agent at Littleton, N. H., and from Apr. 1st, 1880, to Apr. 1st, 1881, agent for the Portsmouth (N. H.) Bell Telephone Co., since which time he has been located at Littleton, N. H., as civil engineer and surveyor, being employed in the location and construction of the Littleton

Water Works, surveying in Bethlehem in connection with the suit of "The N. H. Land Co. *vs.* Henry S. Tilton *et al.*," and other like works. Was Secretary of the Littleton Fire District from March 1st, 1885, to March 1st, 1886. Married, October 23, 1879, at North Haverhill, N. H., to Miss Hattie Ellen, daughter of J. Titus. He is a Republican and a member of the Methodist church, of which he is steward, and recording secretary and treasurer of the Sunday-School. Address, Littleton, N. H.

CHRISTOPHER MARSH GODDARD after graduation accepted position as Instructor in the Higher Mathematics, Chemistry, and Political Science in the Episcopal Academy of Connecticut at Cheshire, Conn., where he also had charge of the Military Department as Commandant, remaining three years, when he re-moved to Brooklyn, N. Y., and was for a short time in the Aud-itor's office of the N. Y., Woodhaven & Rockaway R. R., at Rockaway Beach. In January 1881 entered the employ of Hatch & Foote, bankers, at 12 Wall St., remaining there till their failure in May 1884; was then with Chas. Head & Co. in the same business, and later with the Phoenix Mutual Life Ins. Co. till June 1886, when he accepted the position of Managing Director of the Plainfield District Telegraph and Fire Alarm Co., at Plainfield, N. J., where he had been living since Febru-ary 1882, which position he still holds. Married, February 14, 1882, to Emilie Georgette, daughter of the late George Brand- ner of Brooklyn, N. Y. Has been member of the county and city Republican Executive Committees. Member of City Coun-cil, 1885 to 1887. Is a Mason, being W. of Lodge, P. H. P. of Chapter, and member of Commandery. In politics he is what may be termed a Blainite just now, but always a Republican. Is member of the Crescent Ave. Presby'erian church. Address, Plainfield, N. J.

CHARLES HOWARD HOLMES has been with his father in the undertaking business ever since graduation, but his reports are so brief and far between that I am only able to say he was mar-ried March 7, 1882, and had one child, a boy. Address, Sara-toga Springs, N. Y.

John Jacob Hopper taught in New York city schools from graduation till August 1884, at which time he vice-principal. He then entered the Thayer School of Civil Engineering, Dartmouth College, which he graduated in 1885, when he returned to New York city and acted as Assistant Engineer in the Department of Parks for a while. He then went into contracting business, in which he is still engaged. Married, August 1879; his wife lived but two months. He does not report his politics, but was formerly a Democrat. Address, 163 West 122d St., New York city.

George Isaac McAllister began the study of law with Cross & Burnham, October 1st, 1877, at Manchester, N. H., also with the Hon. David Cross (D. C. '41), and was admitted to the bar in March 1881. He began the practice of law with Hon. H. E. Burnham (D. C. '65) under firm of Burnham & McAllister on April 1st, 1881, which firm was dissolved January 1st, 1884, since which time he has practiced alone. He ran unsuccessfully as the Democratic candidate for County Solicitor in 1884, and made several campaign speeches that year. He was appointed Deputy Collector of Internal Revenue by Hon. Calvin Page, November 1st, 1885, which office he still holds. He has taken the 32d degree in the Scottish Rite, is W. M. of his Lodge, member of Chapter, and S. W. of Trinity Commandery K. T., member of the New Hampshire and the Granite State Clubs. Married, December 22, 1886, to Mattie M., daughter of the late Hon. John M. Hayes. He is a Democrat, and attends the Baptist church. He has made several Memorial Day addresses, and delivered the oration at the dedication of the Soldiers' Monument in Londonderry, N. H., in October 1884. Address, 6 Opera House Block, Manchester, N. H.

Chalmers William Stevens, the son of Walter and Louise (Eames) Stevens, was born at Wentworth, N. H., April 4, 1852, from which place his parents moved to Claremont in the same state, where he fitted in the Stevens High School to enter the Sophomore Class in the Chandler Scientific School of Dartmouth College. After graduation he entered the Thayer School of Civil Engineering in the class of '79. On March 8, 1879, he sailed from New York city for Cordoba, Argentine Republic, *via* Liverpool, to accept a position in the national observatory located there, where he was assistant to Dr. B. A. Gould. While there he gave promise of making his mark as an astronomer, but his career was cut short. On February 16th, 1884, he was instantly killed by a stroke of lightning, while sitting at the breakfast table. He was buried at Cordoba. His is the first and only death among the thirty-four who have been connected with our class in the fourteen years since we entered college.

WILLIAM HENRY VANVLIET after graduation was with Walter McEwan, wholesale dealer in teas, coffees, spices, etc., for two years, since which he has spent his time in traveling about and at Castleton, N. Y., where he is now engaged under the firm name of Budd & VanVliet as pressers of and whole-sale dealers in hay, coal, feed, etc.; they also do a general freighting and forwarding business by the Barge " Ulster Co." Member of Masonic Lodge, Chapter, and Commandery. Married, February 9th, 1887, to Miss Hattie M., daughter of Samuel L. Irish of Malden Bridge, N. Y. He was School Collector and Assistant Town Collector in 1885, is a Mugwump, and member of the Second Presbyterian church of Albany, N. Y. Address, Castleton, N. Y.

NON-GRADUATES.

JAMES AIKEN left college end of freshman year and was employed in his father's machine works at Franklin Falls till the spring of 1880, when he went to Kansas, farming; in fall of 1882 went to Denver, Colo., and in the spring he accepted a position with Sargent & Co. in New Haven, Conn., with whom he remained till the fall of 1885, when he bought a farm in Bridgewater, N. H., where he now makes his home. Married, May 20th, 1880, in New Haven, Conn., to Miss Myra V., daughter of

Nathan W. Cole; has one child, Bertha, born in New Haven, Oct. 24, 1883. He is a Republican. P. O. address, Ashland, N. H.

WILBUR CYRUS ALDRICH left college junior year, and has since devoted himself to the study of law, with Jos. F. Randolph at 120 Broadway, and Hon. Edward Jordan at 234 Broadway, New York city, also to course at Columbia Law School. Ran unsuccessfully as candidate for Board of Education in Jersey City in 1884. Married, August 26th, 1884, to Miss Kate Doty, daughter of P. I. Doty of New York city; they have no children. He reports himself as being a Democrat and an Agnostic. Residence, No. 112 East 113th St. Office, No. 120 Broadway, New York city.

ISAAC BYRON BOUNDS left college in June 1876 and returned to his home at Newark, Ohio, where he entered the drug business in January 1878; sold out in September 1879 and went to Philadelphia, but returned to Newark in June 1881, where he remained till December 1882, when he again returned to Philadelphia to accept a position in the Freight Department of the Penn. R. R. Co., which position he still retains. Married, October 9th, 1878, in Philadelphia, to Miss Carrie Stewart Fine, daughter of Jacob Young Fine; they have one child, William Fine, born July 13th, 1879. He is a member of the Royal Arcanum, a Republican in politics, and attends the Presbyterian church. Residence, No. 512 South 41st St. Office, Empire Line, No. 8 Walnut St., Philadelphia, Penn.

HENRY GEORGE CHANDLER left college junior year, to take a position surveying on the Concord R. R., and since that time has been engaged in various pursuits, but mostly with W. P. Ford & Co. of Concord, N. H., where he now occupies the position of foreman of the Range and Coal Stove Department. He is also connected with A. A. Winkley in the manufacture of artificial legs. Married (1), June 24th, 1885, to Miss Sarah M. Abbott of Concord, who died March 6th, 1886; (2), November 14th, 1886, to Lizzie B. Ferguson of Concord, N. H. Address, 108 South St., Concord, N. H.

ADDISON GARDNER COOK left college at end of sophomore year, and has since that time been in the building material business at Laconia, N. H.; is interested with his father, and also in milling business for himself. Married, October 1st, 1880, to Kate H., daughter of Frederick W. Hathaway of Brockton, Mass.; has had three children, Willie, born May 1883, and Arthur and Louise, born May 1885, of whom Louise has since died. He is an Odd Fellow, and votes the Republican ticket Member of the Unitarian church. Address, Laconia, N. H.

WILLIAM JACOB DAVIS left college end of sophomore year, and remained at his home in Bethel, Vermont, owing to poor health until April 1882, when he went to Concord, N. H., as draughtsman for the Continental Construction Co.; in October of the same year went to work as a machinist for Forsyth & Co. of Manchester, N. H., where he remained until called home by his father's sickness in May 1883. In October 1883 he accepted a position in machine shop of Shortsleeves & Co. of Rutland, Vt., but in June 1886 was again called home by sickness of his father, where he has since remained, carrying on the farm. Married, October 17th, 1877, to Miss Mode, daughter of David W. Cowdery of South Royalton, Vt.; they have one child, Kathrina Mode, born August 28th, 1878. He says: "I am a Republican, dyed in the wool, and a yard wide, warranted to neither rip nor run down at the heel." He is a member of Christ's (Episcopal) church, of which he is one of the vestry, junior warden and treasurer. Address, Bethel, Vt.

FRANK HENRY FISK left college in the fall of 1875 on account of sickness and "went West," to Elgin, Ills., where he was appointed Deputy City Engineer; at the same time commenced the study of law; the next year he secured a position on the Topographical Survey of Montana. He then studied law and did some railroad surveying till the spring of 1878, when he took charge of a graded school at Glenville, Minn., where he remained three years; afterwards was teaching in New Richland and Le Roy, Minn., and now has charge of the schools in Forest City, Iowa. Married in fall of 1880 to Miss Mary, daughter of Henry Thurston of Glenville, Minn. He is, I think, a Republican, as he stumped the county for James G. Blaine, and says he is "ready to do it again."   He is not a church member. Address, Forest City, Winnebago Co., Iowa.

EDWARD S FRANKLIN left college 1875 and returned to Newark, Ohio, where he was engaged in stock raising.   In 1880 he entered into partnership with his brother in queensware business, under firm name of Franklin Bros.; sold out in 1882, and entered the employ of James Cregan & Co., and is now in the employ of M. Q. Baker & Co., dry goods and carpets.   Married, October 4th, 1876, to Miss Florence O., daughter of Judge Geo. M. Grasser, and reports two children, Ruby, born Feb'y 23rd, 1882, and Harold G., born June 13th, 1886.   He is a member of Ahiman Lodge of Newark, O., and Manhattan Commandery of New York city; also of the Royal Arcanum.   He is a Democrat and Episcopalian.   Address, Newark, Ohio.

JOHN HEELEY FRANKLIN left college in December 1875, and accepted the position of teller in the Franklin Bank at Newark, Ohio, where he remained for two years; after that engaged in stock raising, and then in the queensware business with his brother; in 1882 he entered the employ of McCune & Co., as their book-keeper, where he stayed for two years, when he was elected cashier of the People's National Bank of Newark, Ohio, which position he still holds.   He ran unsuccessfully in the spring of 1887 as the Republican candidate for township treasurer, the township having 1300 Democratic majority. Married, August 2nd, 1877, to Miss Helen A., daughter of Henry Sprague, of Newark, Ohio, and has four children, John Henry, born May 4th, 1879, Lillian Helena, March 8th, 1881, Paul, October 11th, 1883, and Robert Rex, November 8th, 1885.   He is a Republican, and a member of the Episcopal church.   Address, care of People's National Bank, Newark, Ohio.

EDMUND BAILEY FRYE left the class in January 1875, when he began the study of medicine in Hanover; in October same year he went to Los Angeles, Cal., remaining there till February 1877, when he returned to Hanover to study with C. P. Frost, M. D., and entered Dartmouth Medical College, gradu-

:ating November 11th, 1879. He began the practice of medicine in Boston, Mass., and in May 1881 removed to Plaistow, N. H., where he continued to practice till November 1885, when he again returned to Boston, where he now is. Married, February 4th, 1880, to Miss Alice E., daughter of Alfred A. Whitney of Boston, and has two children, Mary Alice, born June 22nd, 1881, and Elizabeth Harriet, born June 5th, 1883. Member of the N. H. Medical Society and a Mason. He is naturally a Democrat but of late a Mugwump, and he attends the Unitarian church. Address, 89 Blue Hill Ave., Roxbury, Mass.

SETH NEWTON GAGE left college at end of sophomore year and taught that winter in Pelham, N. H.; he then entered the class of '79, C. S. D., with whom he graduated, after which he taught in Amherst, N. H., and in the spring of 1880, he obtained a position on the engineering corps of the Cincinnati Southern R. R.; in March 1881, he entered the employ of the Mexican National Railway, with whom he filled several important engineering positions. In the spring of 1884 he went to Fort Davis, Texas, and in that fall he accepted the position of secretary and treasurer of the Presidio Live Stock Co., which position he still retains. Married, January 13th, 1886, to Miss Cora C., daughter of John J. Henderson of North Cambridge, Mass. He is a Republican, and attends the Congregational church. Address, Fort Davis, Texas.

EDWARD GOSS HUMPHREY after leaving college returned to St. Johnsbury; in 1877 he was news agent at that place; he was book-keeper in the Flouring Mills of A. H. McLeod, and then with F. F. Fletcher, stoves and hardware; in 1881 he was in the general freight office of the St. Johnsbury & Lake Champlain R. R., where he remained till April 1st, 1885, when he secured a position in the Auditor's office of the Boston & Lowell R. R., at Boston. He has not reported since, but I am informed he has returned to St. Johnsbury. Married, May 16th, 1877, to Miss Almeda D. Hunter, of St. Johnsbury. Address, St. Johnsbury, Vt.

HORACE P. KENT left college in 1875, and in the summer of 1876 was conductor for the Pullman Palace Car Co. between

Boston and Montreal, after which he was engaged for a short time in the Railway Mail Service, and in November 1877 he was appointed to the Naval Office in the U. S. Custom House at Boston, Mass., where he remained until April 1887, when the reform in the Civil Service under the present administration rendered it necessary for him to vacate, since which time he has been rusticating in Portsmouth, N. H. He is a member of Lodge, Chapter, and Commandery of Portsmouth, also of the Sons of Veterans, and in the latter has held the office of Commander of the First Grand Division, comprising the New England States. Married, October 19th, 1880, to Miss Nellie E., daughter of Frank P. Ackerman of Portsmouth, N. H. He is a Republican and a member of the Episcopal church. Address, Box 721, Portsmouth, N. H.

WILLIAM WOODFORD KING left college in January 1874, went to W. Va. till September 1874, when he went to New York city, remaining till April 1875, since which time he has been engaged in railroading, first on the Geneva, Hornellsville & Pine Creek R. R., then with the Canada So. Fast Freight Line at Louisville, Ky., and in December 1877 with the N. Y. Elevated R. R. till February 1880, when he took charge of the construction of the Norfolk Southern at Elizabeth City, N. C., and was appointed train-master of same road in December 1881. In January 1883 was appointed superintendent of construction on the Williamsport & Clearfield R. R. in Penn., and in January 1884 surveyed line for the Iron Belt R. R. in Virginia. In October 1884 accepted position as superintendent of construction on the Ohio River and Lake Erie R. R., which position he resigned in February 1885 to accept the position of train-master of the Norfolk Southern R. R., where he still remains. He is not married, never votes, and has no religious preferences. P. O. address, Berkley, Va.

WILLIAM MORRILL LEAVITT left college at end of freshman year, and began reporting for the Cambridge (Mass.) *Chronicle*, but the east winds of Boston beginning to affect his health he moved to Providence, R. I., and became compositor for the *Journal* of that city, where he remained until about two years ago, when his eyesight and general health became so much impaired that he was obliged to give up regular work. While connected with the *Journal* he made two balloon ascensions on the occasion of the 250th anniversary of the city of Providence. Married, September 15th, 1879, to Miss Ella L., daughter of Thomas M. Himes of Natick, Mass.; his wife died of typhoid fever, November 26th, 1882. Address, Providence, R. I.

FRED LEON PARKER left college at the end of freshman year, and has since been engaged in the drug business in Merrimac, Mass. He was married in 1878 and has no children. He has recently built himself a home, from which and other reports I judge he is being well prospered in his business. Address, Merrimac, Mass.

SYLVIAN MARCELLO RAMSDELL left college in 1876 and entered the Massachusetts Institute of Technology; in 1879 he was in the office of the City Engineer of Lynn; left there and went to St. Louis, Mo., where he entered the employ of Frank H. Pond, mechanical engineer; in June 1881 he accepted the position of engineer in charge of construction Forest Park & Central R. R., and in October same year took charge of a division of the St. Louis & San Francisco R. R. He remained with this road until May 1887, when he was appointed Assistant Chief Engineer of the St. Louis, Arkansas & Texas R. R., where he is now in charge of construction of about 150 miles of new road. Member of the American Society of Civil Engineers. Address, Greenville, Texas.

FRED BATCHELLER SCRIBNER left college during senior year, and studied medicine, first at Hanover and afterwards at the University of the City of New York. In 1880 he was second assistant physican at the New York City Lunatic Asylum on Blackwell's Island, and afterwards first assistant. In January 1882 he took the position of surgeon on the S. S. British Empire, which he held for a short time, then going to the Milwaukee Asylum for the Insane, where in Nov. 1884 he was appointed Superintendent of the Asylum, which position he resigned and began practice in Milwaukee, where he now holds the office of

City Physician.   He reports his business as being largely connected with the courts as an expert in insanity and nervous troubles in criminal cases.   He is a Mason, Knight of Pythias, and a member of the Patriarchal Circle, and a Democrat in politics.   Address, 162 Wisconsin Street, Milwaukee, Wis.

ROBERT RAND SMITH left college in June 1875 and entered the employ of the Chicago Sheffield Steel Works at Chicago, Ills., as salesman and collector.   In May 1876 engaged in the merchandising and mining business as the Co. of Geo. S. Smith & Co. at Lake City, Colorado; from April 1882 to November 1884 travelled for the Pecock Shoe Mfg. Co. of Rochester and Hunt & Holbrook of Hartford, Conn., with headquarters at Denver.   In November 1884 accepted the position of book-keeper in the Bank of Renwick, at Renwick, Iowa, and was in January 1887 appointed cashier and general manager of same bank; is also agent for the Chicago & North West Town Lot Co.   Member City Council, Lake City, Colo., from 1880 to 1882. He is unmarried, a Republican, and member of Episcopal church.   Address, Renwick, Iowa.

RUSSELL ALLEN WENTWORTH left college before graduation, but returned and entered the class of '79 in the fall of 1877, with whom he graduated.   He then was with the engineer corps of the Buffalo Div. of the N. Y., L. E. & W. R. R. for a year, and then for fifteen months in the gold fields of the Black Hills. In October 1881 he returned to the Erie R. R., in whose employ he remained till December 1883, when he secured his present position as engineer of the Dagus Mines.   In 1884 he made a complete topographical map of the Dagus Mines, which was published with the Report of the Second Geological Survey of Cameron, Elk, and Forest Counties, Penn.   Married, · March 13th, 1884, to Miss Lizzie A., daughter of the Hon. John Tubbs of Osceola, Penn.; he has one child, Edward Tubbs, born December 24th, 1884.   His wife died July 26th, 1885.   He is a member of the Knights and Ladies of Honor, a Republican, and a member of the Congregational church of Salmon Falls, N. H. Address, Dagus Mines, Elk Co., Penn.

FREDERICK WILLIAM WHITE left college in November 1873, and entered the High School in Burlington, Vermont; in spring of 1874 entered the dry goods store of Lyman & Allen, and in August 1876 accepted a position with the Burlington Woolen Co., at Winooski, Vermont, remaining with them till 1883, when he was paymaster and senior in the office. In September 1883 he accepted the position of book-keeper and financial manager for Gibson, Miller & Richardson, printers, binders and lithographers at Omaha, Nebraska, which position he still holds. Married, March 22nd, 1882, to Miss Josie, daughter of Samuel Schofield of Winooski, Vt.; they have had two children, Vernon Schofield, born June 16th, 1883, and Mary Annette, born July 31st, 1886, died October 26th, 1886. He is a member of the C. L. S. C., and of a Masonic Lodge, Chapter, and Council, in which he has held various offices, and has taken the 14th degree of the Scottish Rite. He is a Republican, a member of the Seward M. E. church of Omaha, has held the office of recording steward, is now one of the trustees, and has also been class leader, chorister, librarian, etc., of the same church. Address, 2902 Yates St., Omaha, Nebraska.

CHARLES SEWARD WILCOX left college in January 1875, and was a clerk in Cleveland, Ohio, for a while; then in September 1876 he entered the Sheffield School, Yale College, and graduated in class of 1879; in July same year he entered the employ of the Ontario Rolling Mill Co. of Hamilton, Ont., in which company he now holds the position of second vice-president and treasurer. He attends the church of England. Address, Hamilton, Ontario.

RECORD OF CLASS REUNIONS.

TRIENNIAL REUNION, 1880.

Fifteen men assembled for a formal business meeting at the Senior Recitation Room, in Dartmouth Hall, at 6:45 P. M., Wednesday, June 23. Those present were Campbell, Carpenter, Comstock, Goddard, Howe, W. H. Ray, Robinson, Saunderson, J. H. Smith, Temple, Thombs, Tillotson, A. Wallace, C. A. Willard, W. J. Willard. Tillotson presided, being the last chosen Vice-President. Brown had been in town early in the week, but left before the meeting. The class cup was on exhibition, having been procured in Boston by Temple, and after the meeting was forwarded by express to the recipient, Master Nelson Pierce Brown.

It was voted, that annual reports be printed for the next five years, and also a report in 1887. A balance in the treasury of about $50 was reported, and a tax of one dollar was levied for the expense of future reports. The next reunion was voted to be held on Wednesday of commencement week in 1887, and Robinson, Comstock, and Carpenter were appointed by the chair as a committee of arrangements.

The meeting was adjourned to 8 o'clock on Thursday morning. At that time the resignation of VanVliet as Scientific Secretary was received and accepted, and Goddard was appointed to fill the vacancy. The roll of the class was called, and information concerning the absent was supplied as far as possible.

There was no formal class meeting from 1880 to 1887, but the number of '77 men present at the commencements of 1883 and 1885 deserves mention here. In 1883, Brown, Carpenter, Carrigan, Cooper, Farnsworth, Robinson, and Tillotson were in Hanover; and in 1885, Brown, Campbell, Carpenter, Carrigan, Comstock, Farnsworth, Hammond, Leslie, H. L. Moore, and Robinson.

DECENNIAL REUNION, 1887.

Primus Moore was first on the ground, arriving the week before commencement with wife and two children. Cooper was the next to appear. Both were rewarded for their promptness, Moore acting as marshal on commencement day, and Cooper as one of the judges at prize speaking. Each train on Tuesday and Wednesday brought some of the class. Goddard and Primus Chase came with their wives. Changes of personal appearance in some cases were so striking and unexpected that laughable failures to recognize each other were not uncommon. We missed some whom we had expected to see, but all went away thoroughly glad they came. At 9 o'clock on Wednesday evening we sat down to the supper at Conant Hall. Moore, as toast-master, presided through most of the evening. Grace was said by Sewall. We were arranged at the tables in the following order, beginning at Moore and going toward the right : Moore, Sewall, Campbell, I. A. Chase, Patten, Thombs, Deane, Goddard, McAllister, Montgomery, Carrigan, Noxon, Temple, Brown, Owen, J. H. Smith, Cooper, Saunderson, Cook, W. J. Willard, C. A. Willard, Merriam, Carpenter, Comstock,—twenty-four in all.

During the evening the following telegram was read :

"New York, N. Y. To Philip Carpenter, Conant Hall.— The orator and poet of '77 have just drunk the health of their classmates at Delmonico's, and send most cordial greetings to you all.

(Signed)
WILLIAM G. DAVIS and LEWIS ROSENTHAL."

After the discussion of the edibles, Noxon and Carpenter read what purported to be a history of the class for the ten years, and Owen read a poem, after which the toast-master called upon Cooper, C. A. Willard, Goddard, Brown, Montgomery, Carrigan, and Smith. We finally adjourned at about one o'clock.

The following business was transacted during the evening. A balance of about $30 was reported in the treasury, and a tax of $1.50 was raised, to cover the expense of this Decennial Record, and of such other printing as should be done before the next reunion. The Secretaries were directed to print annually a directory similar to the one sent out last January, and more extended reports at their discretion. Reunions were appointed at Hanover for the commencements of 1892 and 1897, and Brown, Carrigan, and McAllister were appointed a committee of arrangements for 1892, Comstock to act with them as Secretary. The committee were also empowered to call and arrange for a reunion in Boston at any time they may think fit.

JOHN M. COMSTOCK, *Secretary.*